Addicted To You

A BWWM Alpha Male BBW Enemies To Lovers Romance

Kylie Hudson

*Dedicated to my loving family, (Heth and Bogie) thanks for
all your patience and support.
You are my inspiration.*

Contents

DESCRIPTION

Whit is chiseled and muscle-wrapped but with a face that could belong to a male model.

Surely not the features you would expect from a Mafia hitman.

He lives a life of secrecy and shadow, blood and money.

But his latest assignment leaves a sour taste in his mouth after he meets his target…innocent and beautiful beyond compare.

Yes, the kind of woman a man could easily become addicted to.

Khloe,

Innocent.

Naïve.

Romantic.

Ready for her wedding night with the man of her dreams.

But all that changes when she comes face-to-face with the hot Alpha Male sent to cut short her honeymoon short.

And her idyllic world comes crashing down, as she discovers a dangerous truth.

Addicted To You, formerly published as "Taken by the Mafia Hit Man", has been re-edited and a number of new paragraphs and epilogues added. It's a steamy, standalone, erotic BBW Romance with a HEA ending. No cliffhangers.

If you enjoy this book, please leave a review to help other readers discover this author's works.

Chapter 1

Whit

My foot crashes against the wooden door, smashing it open.

The man seated on the sofa, taking a sip of his beer, jumps to his feet, alarmed at my untimely entrance.

His hand reaches under the sofa. But he is too late. Like a panther, I hurdle across the room and knock him to the floor.

"Motherfucka," the hulking black man screams, blood spewing from his busted lip.

But to no avail. He is looking up at the nozzle of my Glock 26.

I see the fear imprinted in his eyes. "What … what do you want?" he stammers, cold sweat washing over his bearded face.

"Your fucking life," I answer icily.

"No. No, wait...I have money...I have coke. You can take it all." I see the terror in his eyes. The all too familiar look of a man who realizes his days are numbered. A look I have seen so many times before on the faces of the men I have sent to their graves.

"It's too late for that." My finger gently squeezes the trigger, popping two rounds into his skull.

His lifeless body slumps to the floor.

I rummage through his pockets and take the large coil of hundred-dollar bills. The cocaine is on the kitchen table, about 2 kilos - one in a large container, the other stored in small dime bags. Seems my target was in the process of bagging them for sale. I take all the coke too.

The idea was to make the contract killing of this drug dealer look like a deal gone bad. The Mafia Dons who control this area of the Bronx don't take kindly to an upstart peddling his wares in their territory.

I nonchalantly step over the body and walk out into the cool New York night air, as if nothing had just happened.

Yeah, I'm a Mafia hitman. I kill people for money.

Just call me Whit. In my business, there are no names, just aliases.

And my clients say that I'm the best in the business.

Remorse?

Hell no. Most of the scumbags I put away deserve it anyway.

Innocent victims? No one is really innocent. And if they are, that's just their tough luck. Casualties of war, I say.

I live my life on the wrong side of the law, and I'd be one of the most wanted men alive, given the kills under my belt. Twenty-two to be exact.

But no one knows who I really am.

Not the Feds, the CIA, the mob, or even my employers. I'm what you call a freaking ghost;

That's the reason I've been able to stay the fuck alive for so long. As a hitman, I live a life of secrecy and shadows; blood and money.

My clients have all been satisfied customers and none of my targets have lived to tell the tale.

But of late, I have been feeling restless though.

Sometimes I think about giving up the game.

But what would I do - get a wife and kids and live in the suburbs?

No. Not for me, I would die of boredom. Besides, I love fucking different chicks too much and in my line of business, you just can't afford to get too close to a woman…you lose your edge, and once that happens, it's the beginning of the end.

So what else would I do with my life?

I had always been intrigued by death, which made me the perfect killing machine while being a member of the elite Navy Seals. But after being discharged following a clash with an officer – I knocked his fucking teeth out - I was introduced into the world of assassins by a close friend who knew of my special skills.

No, I'm content. I've gone too far to turn back.

I smile at a pretty young dark-skinned girl as she passes by. Her eyes sparkle and she returns my smile. Any other night and I would probably stop and try to pick her up. But not tonight; my blood is hot…piping hot.

It's always this way after a kill. I get hot and lustful.

What can I say I'm a fucking scumbag…a cold-hearted bastard with no goodness inside of me. Blood flows through my veins, but I have no soul.

I walk for a long time, taking in the sights of New York's lowliest borough. I'm feeling restless. An upcoming job is leaving a bitter taste in my mouth.

A local mob boss has contracted me to kill his wife on their wedding night...making it look like an accident.

Can you believe it; their fucking wedding night? The guy couldn't even wait a year or something. Some people are fucking warped.

Still, it could very well be the perfect crime. No one would expect a man to have his wife murdered on their wedding night.

Fuck, I don't mind killing, but snapping the neck of a poor, defenseless girl is certainly not my idea of a gig. Dammit, it's a lot of money and to refuse would cause a ton of heat on my head, something I definitely can't afford.

Yet, I hesitate It was a strange request.

As usual, I received an email in my untraceable account. Untraceable because I have my email addresses routed through several servers all around the world, so they are impossible to trace. Thanks to one of my computer geeks, no one in the world can find me.

The job was for a large sum, three hundred

grand in fact, well above my normal fee of two hundred grand a hit. So I had been intrigued, imagining having to take out some high-profile target. Then I discovered it was from a New York gangster and I was to make it look like his millionaire heiress wife took her own life, stricken by the grief of her father's recent death.

There are several ways I could do the job. Simply make it look like she slipped on the wet floor and broke her neck, or maybe a scenario where she knocked a curling iron into her bath. Something tragic. Something that would make her scumbag husband appear the heartbroken widower.

Then he'd get his payday, and we'd both walk away from this happy. He, with his millions in blood money and I with a cool bounty, that could send me to some exotic Caribbean island for a couple of weeks to fuck all the native girls I could.

For some reason, I grimace as I think about her.

Khloe Spencer.

Like most jobs, I spend a lot of time casing out the target. But this time… whoa… damn. The first time I saw her, the fucking world almost stopped spinning. I kid you not. She is one of the most gorgeous creatures God has ever placed on this earth.

Khloe is tall, about five-ten, but curvy as hell.

Not your slim, model-type doll. The girl has meat on her bones. Her tits are ripe and inviting. The type a man imagines resting his head against or sinking his teeth into while banging the shit out of her. Her busty top descends into a tiny waist and again flares out into thick, broad hips.

You get the picture now.

Sorry. I forgot to mention her ass. Jeez, a trunk that you could place a glass on and it would not fall. Add bewitching eyes and shoulder-length hair and you come up with an unbeatable combination.

And the guy wants to murder that entire bundle of joy? was the first thought that sprang through my mind. If I had a girl like that I would want to fuck her every night for the rest of my life, much less kill her.

What is the damn world coming to?

I've been watching her from afar, studying her, so I'd know what would seem like the most likely accident. Yet the doubts keep creeping up into my head. Yeah, I've had to take the life of a few people who maybe didn't deserve it, but never a target as innocent, alluring, and captivating as Khloe. Something about her has touched a chord inside me... a chord I didn't even think I possessed anymore.

She has a way of smiling with people that makes them go soft in her company and she is always bubbly and kind, even to strangers.

The girl gives away money to homeless people she meets on the street for Christ's sake. Even when she shops for clothes, she tips the salespersons. It's hard to find a fault with Miss Spencer.

To think that she has been deceived by a mobster without her even knowing what he did for a living kinda galls me.

The day before her wedding and the kill, I decided to get close to her, just that one once. She was buying hot dogs from one of the street vendors in Manhattan when I sidled up beside her and ordered one too. My features were well-disguised with dark glasses and a fake beard, so there was no chance of her recognizing me again, not that it mattered since she would be dead.

Khloe had smiled at me as I ordered…the million-watt smile that simply lights up the world.

"It's so good, don't you think?" She had commented, flashing a smile. "Maybe I should buy another."

I had just smiled back at her, nodded my head, and started moving away. But for a moment my feet were stuck in quicksand. I stared into her eyes, drinking in her beauty. She simply stared back, grinning from ear-to-ear.

She just had an innocence and vitality about her; the exact opposite of creeps like me.

As I walked away, something snapped. How fucking unfair is life, that the cutthroat mob boss Jason Gray, who had killed her father, could then steal the unwitting girl's fortune?

Chapter 2

Whit

I have a few hours before I have to hit my new target, and I'm sitting in a local singles bar watching the girls flash their nubile bodies around, trying to attract me. I tell you, they are on the prowl tonight. Take the curvy black temptress ensconced in the corner, her melons jutting out invitingly. Or just look at the waif-like white seductress sitting at the bar close to me.

Get the picture? The smell of carnal desires is permeating the fucking air. You can almost taste it. If you're a red-blooded male in this joint tonight and you can't get laid you may as well be fucking dead.

The strange thing is I always feel horny before a kill. It's like the thrill of a bloodlust just drives up my sexual appetite.

A quick random fuck normally slows down

the adrenalin flowing through my body, putting me in just the right calm state of mind.

Grabbing the glass of whiskey, I toss it down my throat. The liquid burns, but feels good going down. This assignment is starting to leave a bad taste in my mouth. Regardless, I'm a pro and I have to go through with it. My reputation is on the line here.

I need a good fuck. Not a plain boring missionary bedroom fuck.

I need some nasty, dark fucking encounter with a girl not afraid to be naughty. Honestly, I don't normally go for African American chicks, but after meeting Khloe for some warped reason I want to sample some exotic pussy tonight.

The curvy, dark girl sitting in the corner looks like a likely candidate. She should make a good substitute for the super-hot Miss Spencer.

She's been giving me the eye all evening, so I rise from my spot at the bar and nonchalantly saunter over to where she is sitting alone, plopping myself on the chair beside her. "Is this seat taken or is it reserved for me?" I flash my bad boy smile, staring her straight in the eyes as if trying to peer into her soul. Her eyes are wet and mysterious, accentuated by long lashes.

"Free country," she smiles, batting those long lashes. "What took you so long?"

"I didn't want to look like one of your cheap, eager fucks."

"Oh my, you certainly are a naughty boy who deserves a spanking." She licks her lips in a lascivious manner and her eyes pop open wider.

"Let's get one thing clear; I do the spanking and fucking here…Miss…?"

She gently nibbles on her bottom lip. "Benson…Lydia Benson," she says in a New York accent.

Without warning, I grab her wrist hard, leaving no doubt as to who is in charge. "Here's how it's going to play out Lydia…you're going to go to the ladies' room and I will follow in five minutes. I'll knock and if the coast is clear, you're going to open the door. You got that Miss Lydia Benson?"

"Shit…" Lydia blurts out, her breaths coming out in short gasps. "You are not serious, Mr…"

"Just call me Whit…And do I look like the kind of man who jokes around to you?"

Lydia swings back her head, her flowing hair tossing from side to side. Moving closer, I place my hand on her thighs. She flinches in anticipation but doesn't pull away.

My fingers creep up her thighs until I can feel her skimpy, lace panties. Detecting dampness, I yank the material to one side, slip a finger inside, and gently stroke the folds of her damp pussy. Lydia's body jolts and even in the dim light, I make out the hunger in her eyes. Her strong thighs squeeze against my finger, holding it in its present position.

I continue stroking her pussy lips while she slowly grinds her hips. Then my finger flicks on her clit causing her to jerk upright, a hungry moan escaping her lips. Her panties are becoming flooded with her love juices. "You are driving me half-crazy, Whit," she snorts breathily. "I love the way you stroke my clit."

"You haven't seen anything get, woman." My index finger darts inside her wet cunt and she lets out a yelp, reaches down, and grabs my crotch.

"Time to go to the ladies' room," I command, my eyes burning into her. The pert nipples on her chest have stiffened considerably, causing my cock to harden inside my pants.

Lydia gets up obediently, straightens her mini-skirt, and disappears from view.

My cock is now standing at attention and I watch as her sexy ass beat a Brazilian samba while she walks away.

Waiting five minutes and downing another shot of whiskey, I head towards the ladies' bathroom. It's a classy kinda joint, so the piss houses are big and spacious. I knock once and immediately the door opens. Inside I see sexy ass Lydia gesturing seductively toward me.

Backing her into one of the stalls, I pull her trembling body up to mine and my mouth covers her, wanting her sighs, taking them. My hungry lips rain hot kisses fuelled by forbidden desires.

My mouth commands hers to obey.

Her mouth is warm and feminine, her breath sweet, and my dark, sexy conquest locks her hands around my neck and returns my kisses…real hard.

Her lips taste like strawberries. I can smell her too. Her scent is that of a woman aroused. Her sexual aroma is filling up the stall, causing my cock to try and bore a hole in my pants.

I feel her foraging tongue pushing past my lips, seeking mine. I respond. Our savage tongues circle like two snakes saying hello.

"Fuck, your lips are hot, they have me wetting my panties." A hum of satisfaction slips from her lips. Bolting the door to the stall her greedy fingers reach for my zipper, sliding it down in a flash and search for the fleshy object inside. Lydia presses closer making a low, throaty sound of pleasure.

My erect cock springs mercifully free from the prison in my pants and Lydia grabs it by the base and slowly begins fisting me. "Fuck," I hiss, cum bubbling up in my balls. "Yeah baby, stroke that cock." My dick is growing, filling up her hands. Lydia pulls me closer to her, my arousal pressing her belly.

Listen, in case you didn't know, public sex is the ultimate turn-on for an Alpha male. The thought of fucking someone while other people are nearby, or there's a chance at being caught, makes my blood boil.

Locked in the ladies' room with this hot temptress, I immediately spring into action. Hands shaking with need I undo the zipper at the back of her little dress and watch it slide down her body. Lydia isn't wearing a bra and the sight of her ripe nipples causes my breathing to get ragged in a hurry. The girl is fine as fuck.

Instinctively I cup her breasts, squeezing the dark globes hard, causing her to wince. "You've got some tits on you," I rasp. "Can't wait to rub my cock between them."

"You are a very bad boy." Lydia's nipples are distended. My thumb flicks over them and she shivers. I run my tongue up and down her nipples and they stiffen even harder. They are the size of small coins, I kid you not. Her eyes are closed and her breathing harsh. I cover one breast with my mouth and bite on it. Lydia lets out a muffled scream. "I want you to fuck me, Whit," she moans wantonly, causing the hairs on the back of my neck to stand up. A vein ticks ominously in my temple.

There's no time to savor the bountiful physical attributes of this thick woman, since I have a girl to kill in a few hours, plus this bathroom is sure to start getting busy soon. I tug her dress down, watching it fall to the floor, and my eyes nearly pop out of my head at the sight of her voluptuous curves. Lust sweeps through my core and in one swift motion I tear her panties off her hips and stuff them into my pocket, a shredded memento on this night of passion.

"Whit, you are a beast," Lydia grunts, her eyes clouded in a sexual haze. My brutal carnality seems to have turned her on even more, as lets out a loud moan and pushes again me, fire imprinted on her irises.

"Shut the fuck up, bitch," I snarl into her ear, before sinking my teeth into her neck, nibbling on her hot skin. "Do you want the whole world to know we are fucking up in here?"

"No...no," she sighs, almost apologetically. Then her voice drops an octave and I can feel the trembling excitement in her words. "But I want you to fuck me now, Whit. Take me now. I want your big fucking cock in my wet pussy," she whines, a sense of urgency in her voice.

My finger trails down her flat tummy, her body whispering like silk against mine, until I grab hold of her pussy, feeling the pronounced folds pulsating against my fingers. Fuck, I can't wait to feel my cock nestled between her pussy lips while I thrust into her. "Spread your legs," I command, prying open her legs. Lydia whimpers as I fondle her wide-open pussy. Fuck, my balls are loaded to the point of bursting.

Blowing a hot breath, my finger discovers her wet, slippery nub and begins stroking it. Lydia bites into my shoulders. "If you keep on playing with that little girl I am going to cum too soon....please, Whit, I want to cream on your cock." Her legs begin shaking and she digs her long, sharp talons into my shoulder. "Fuck man, I want you inside me...please-eee Whit," Lydia begs. There is a tortured look on her face.

But, being a dominant male, I remain in total control, teasing her snatch until she is rotating her hips against my fingers, trying to pull them deeper inside. Lydia is like a bitch in heat and finally, it is time to give her a just reward. I press her against the bathroom stall, grab her hips, hoisting her up and while watching the fire in her eyes, roll on a condom and gently rub my dick against her damp folds. Fuck, these lips are heavenly, and it takes all my willpower not to nut all over her flesh.

Damn it, Lydia's pussy feels unbelievably tight. When my cock is sufficiently moist from her juices, then I roughly turn her face toward the wall, slap her and force my cock inside her inviting slit. "Whit....whit..." she gurgles, eyes bulging and face pressing against the wall. "Your cock is so big, you are filling me up."

The excitement of having sex in a ladies' bathroom has my shaft as turgid like a piece of cast iron. Plunge my cock into her pussy causes Lydia to gasp. The scent of a new pussy is intoxicating and heady. For a thick girl, she is so damn tight, almost like a virgin. For a bar-hopper, this gal hasn't been fucked a lot.

Just my lucky day.

This dark pussy is so darn good.

My cock feels like it belongs inside her cunt. Again and again, I pump into her quivering flesh and she grunts like a stuck pig. Her hand reaches backward, grabs my ass, and pulls me in until all my cock is buried to the hilt. I can feel the fucking walls of her pussy clenching against me, wanting to rob me of my cum juice.

Lydia backs up her amazing ass against me, bends down until her hands are touching her toes, and screws me in a clockwise movement. Can you fucking believe it, this girl is a veritable fuck toy.

Man, listen, I have great control when I fuck. I can hang in a long time and mix it up in the tightest pussy, but this girl is good. The grinding number her hips are doing on her has me hanging on for dear life.

I have to think about work...about all the things I hate, to keep from busting my nut inside her.

There is something freaky about pubic sex. The feeling is off the damn chain. For those who have never experienced it before, half of your life is fucking gone. You need to get your rocks off out in the open, man. The thrill of knowing that at any moment someone could come in and discover you sliding your rod into a wet pussy makes it the ultimate sex act. Fuck bondage – sex in public is the mother of all kinkiness.

My cock thrusts into Lydia the tendons in my neck standing out in sharp relief. "Fuck the shit out of me," she raps, arching her hips and meeting me thrust for thrust. "I want you to fuck my pussy raw, baby." Each stroke of my cock is harder than the next, but she matches my speed and grunts furiously. My teeth bite into the back of her neck, which I am sure will leave a hickey tomorrow. But I don't give a damn. I jaw against her jugular and her body goes crazy, almost collapsing.

Lydia bits her lips to keep from screaming as pleasure knifes through her body and just as she is about to cum, we hear footsteps entering the bathroom. Lydia and I cease our movements... not daring to breathe, lest we attract attention. My cock is still embedded in her pussy, throbbing and swelling as her sex clenches and unclenches.

I hear two voices. One woman enters a stall, while the other appears to be washing her hands and applying makeup. I kiss Lydia's neck and gently rotate my erect organ inside her. I feel her flesh quivering, knees buckling, so I hold on to her waist and place my hand over her mouth to stop her from crying out.

Mercifully, the intruders finish their business quickly.

As they exit the bathroom, my dick knifes into Lydia again and again, her passage quaking at my onslaught. Sweat crawls down my forehead like a slithering snake and I pump her deeper, stretching her cunt. "You are fucking making me cum." She bites on my finger. I feel her channel melting around my cock, bathing me in her feminine juices. A tidal wave smacks her and Lydia overflows her banks. She stiffens again as another orgasm washes over her.

Plunging into her one last time, I grab her ass and shoot my load inside her. The thought of snapping Khloe's neck in a few hours has given me extra power, and I flood inside the condom.

I gently withdraw from inside her just as Lydia's orgasm begins to recede.

"Enjoy the rest of your evening," I mutter in her ear, pull up my pants and zipper, and beat a hasty retreat from the ladies' room.

The male bathroom is nearby, so I walk inside and examine myself in the mirror. I splash cold water on my face and towel it dry.

Come on Whit, time to go. Time to make a quick three hundred thousand bucks. It's time for me to wrap my hands around Khloe's delicate little neck and snuff her life out.

I exit the singles bar into the cool of the night, feeling like my normal self. Nothing calms a man more than a good fuck with a sexy, nubile chick and I'm no different in that regard.

Still, after twenty-two kills, this next seems different, trivial maybe, but the fact is I know I have no choice. In my business, a broken contract means the end of the line.

The Paradise Hotel is a few blocks away, so I decide to talk. On reaching the rather posh building, I enter from the service entrance and after picking the lock, sneak up into the honeymoon suite.

Now all I have to do is stand and wait for pretty Miss Spencer to finish her wedding reception and retire for the night. Her hubby will remain at the reception a bit longer, mingling with his guests and creating the perfect alibi.

Khloe will have a rude awakening. Instead of hot, steamy honeymoon sex, it will be her very own funeral that awaits.

Chapter 3

Khloe

I'm trying to squeeze my curvy body into my stunning wedding gown.

A few of my friends and acquaintances are gathered around me, tittering about how beautiful I look, how lucky my husband is going to be, and how happy they all are for me.

Gail Thompson, my bestie from college days and my wing girl, gushes with pride, her lovely blue eyes flashing. "Girl, you are rocking that dress." You would almost believe she is the one getting married, such is her obvious excitement.

I twirl around, shaking my booty. "You don't say, honey!" Having my friends around has put a pep in my step, on what would normally be a stressful day.

The funny thing is though, as I stare at myself in the full-length mirror, I don't recognize the person staring back at me.

Yes, I see a black, curvy, beautiful girl, with long, dark hair streaked with gold, and eyes that everyone says are brown and pretty. But I'm worried… worried that my heart isn't in the same place as my body. I am just not feeling all that beautiful inside.

I should be happy – over the moon actually. Which girl wouldn't be on her wedding day? This should be the greatest day of my life. The one that every bright-eyed, young black girl dreams of from the moment she first starts noticing boys.

Still, my thoughts are cloudy.

Am I getting married for the right reasons?

My mind flashes back to the death of my beloved father, Marlon Spencer, a man whom I loved with all my heart and soul. He was the subject of my little-girl adoration. For as long as I could remember daddy was my hero.

I remember that fateful day as if it just happened a few moments ago, at the funeral when the man who was to become my fiancé, Jason Gray, approached me. "You are much too pretty to cry… here, take my handkerchief and wipe away those tears," Jason said, flashing that cute smile of his. "And my shoulder is here to lean on, just in case you decide to cry some more."

My eyes had looked up, and man, you should have seen him…dashing and rather handsome. He appeared much more sympathetic and tender than I realized he could be, back then. One thing led to another and without knowing what hit me I began seeing him.

I won't lie. At first, it was amazing. I was flattered at being on the receiving end of a romantic courtship from this exciting and fun, albeit slightly older than myself, self-assured man.

Jason literally swept me off my feet.

We had an amazing courtship, and then presto, after I agreed to marry him, the romance all but vanished.

No, *he* vanished.

The Jason Gray I had come to know and love just disappeared into thin air, replaced by a stranger who I hardly recognized anymore.

Yes, once he proposed and I accepted, Jason started acting like he wasn't excited about marrying me at all – disappearing for days at a time without checking in with me and hardly taking me out in public. All the small things he used to do to show me he loved me dried up.

I shake my head in frustration, as my thoughts return to the present.

So I'm having doubts, but which girl on her wedding day doesn't? We all wonder if we are marrying Mr. Right, don't we?

"Time to get you down the aisle, Khloe," Joey Martin, the best man, approaches me with a smile. Joey is one of Jason's business partners and with my fiancé so often absent, we have grown to be close friends. I can say without a doubt that he's got my back.

The sight of the affable Joey causes my mood to lighten, and I slip back into the character of the blushing bride.

"I'm ready, Joey," I gush, winking in his direction.

"Oh my goodness!" Joey blurts out, his eyes roving from my head to toe. "Aren't you the most beautiful bride I have ever seen?"

"Flattery will get you nowhere." I blush. "I bet you say that to all the brides."

Joey takes my hand and leads me outside the room. "Never...because there is only one Khloe Spencer... and she is the most beautiful woman in the world."

The murmurings from the audience gathered in the large hotel barroom where the wedding is to take place filters to my ears, so I suck in extra air.

This is it Khloe. This is your big day.

A sigh escapes my lips, as I try to convince myself that things will be back to normal with Jason once the ceremony is over.

No better than normal. Out of this world, even.

No need to be jittery, Khloe.

Joey guides me by the hand to the nerve-wracking holding area, just before we walk down the aisle. In the distance, I can see the beautiful floral decorations inside the reception room – Decorations that my girls and I had personally chosen.

Suddenly, however, just before we turn the corner to face the crowd, Joey stops and pulls me aside. "Joey, what's the matter?" I enquire nervously, concerned by this unusual display. "Why are we stopping?"

The Best Man looks at me forlornly. A hint of fear and concern creases his handsome face. "I have something to tell you, Khloe. And look, I'm taking a big chance here, so you have to promise never to tell anyone I told you."

My heart is doubling or tripling in speed. "What is it, Joey? You are starting to scare me." As if I didn't have enough nervousness going through with the wedding, Joey has some big secret to tell me.

Talk about crappy timing.

Joey's eyes are wild and erratic, looking everywhere but at my face. This is now really starting to freak me out.

He nervously wipes his brow. "Khloe, I would feel guilty for the rest of my life if I didn't tell you."

"What Joey. What? The wedding is about to start." Is the Best Man really going to tell me that my husband is a cheat right now?

Joey takes a deep breath, his eyes scanning the room as if to make sure there's no one within earshot. "Jason, your loving husband-to-be, is going to have you killed tonight after the wedding, and make it look like an accident."

Pain shoots through my heart and it feels like it is about to explode or catch fire. My jaw feels like a spring wound with tension. I try to speak, but the words hitch in the back of my throat.

I feel faint like my knees are about to buckle and I have to brace against Joey to keep from falling. "What do you mean have me killed? Joey, if this is your idea of a sick joke, or to stop me from marrying Jason, well it isn't funny."

"I'm deadly serious. Don't ask me how I know all this, but Jason has contracted a top-level hitman to take your life tonight in the honeymoon suite." His eyes harden and I finally realize that Joey isn't joking. "Khloe, you have to get away. You have to disappear now and never come back, or you're a dead woman."

Caught between a feeling of fear and disbelief I hesitate for a moment. My world is crashing down right before my eyes. What if Joey is telling the truth? Suppose he is doing all this to break up Jason and me? After all, he told me not to tell about his revelations.

"Listen Khloe, I'm telling you this for your own safety. Hell, I'm putting my neck on the chopping block here," Joey snaps. "If you go through with the wedding, Jason's going to kill you for your inheritance and take it for himself. It's all been a plan… this was all about marrying you, and then with you out of the picture, the money will be all his."

But Jason is a very successful businessman, so my inheritance shouldn't make all that much difference to him, or would it?

My thoughts again flash back to the past several weeks. Could I have unwittingly put my life, and my heart, into the wrong hands? Had I been just a naive twenty-one-year-old girl, too star-struck and grieving to see the truth in front of me?

Jason was an older, powerful man and an old business acquaintance of my father, who swept me off my feet in a whirlwind romance; offering me comfort, then protection, and eventually, what I presumed to be love. All that had transpired after dad died leaving me as the sole beneficiary of his estate and millions in his will. Had this all been too good to be true?

Jason had bowled me over with his knowledge, charm, and worldliness. He knew everyone and all the right places to take me - always introducing me as his girl. Of course, I had been overwhelmed that a man like him could have fallen in love with an innocent young girl like me.

It had all happened so fast and in a matter of weeks, I had found myself engaged to him.

But once we became engaged, something about Jason changed. He became very pushy about the wedding, trying to push up the date, forcing me to wonder what all the rush was for.

Trying to push my apprehension away, I threw my entire passion and energy into planning the perfect wedding, even as my heart began to ache. Now, I wonder if all of that had just been a way for me to cope with the loneliness of losing my dad...the last of my immediate family.

So what are you going to do Khloe, your husband-to-be awaits?

Chapter 4

Khloe

My knees are shaking as I walk down the aisle to the strains of "Here Comes the Bride".

After Joey told me about the plot against my life, I had pondered my options. Should I run? There was no way I would be able to find a way to leave the church undetected and there's nowhere I could go for safety.

So I decide to go through with the wedding and hope to God that Joey had been wrong, or just being plain mischievous.

As I stroll down the aisle, I glance up at my fiancé standing beside the minister with a big smile on his face. Or is that a smirk I see? He appears dashing enough and looking at him you wouldn't believe he is thirty-five. Most of my friends had asked what I saw in him since he was much older, but I laughed it off that age was just a number.

Finally, I reach the rest of the bridal party and the Minister begins the ceremony. The entire event seems to pass like a haze in front of me. I hear the Minister's words and recite my vows, but the ceremony appears to be something out of a dream.

Even when Jason kisses me after we are pronounced man and wife, I still feel numb. I look in his eyes and all I can think of is, yes *now that we are married, are you still going to have me killed?*

Everyone seems to be having a good time, both at the wedding and at the lavish reception that follows afterward in the ballroom. Everyone that is, but me. I'm too filled with anxiety and trepidation. For his part, Jason spends most of his time chatting with his boys and getting pats on the back.

Eventually, the party draws to a close, and finally free to disappear, I accost Jason.

I give him a peck on the lips. "Husband, I'm going to retire to the honeymoon suite, are you coming."

Joey's crew all start slapping him on the back and making snide remarks. "Not yet, darling, I have a few friends to talk to and keep the party going." He smiles at me. "But you go ahead, get all dolled up in something sexy for me and I'll join you as soon as I can." With those words, he plants a paternal kiss on my cheek and again focuses his attention on the boys.

Judas? The kiss of death?

I had been hoping with all my heart Jason would have left the party with me. That would have dispelled all my fears. Now, I'm not so sure. Is it that he wants me alone in the suite?

I*s he really going to have me killed?*

Dragging myself out of the hotel's ballroom, I slowly climb into the elevator and punch the number for the penthouse. It's the longest elevator ride of my life, seeming to take hours rather than a few seconds. Finally, I disembark and swipe my key to enter the room. So many emotions are running through my mind. I'm praying that Joey is wrong, but deep down I know in my heart that he wasn't lying, after all, why would he be making up some sick joke like that, and on my wedding day at that?

The suite is dark, so I reach for the switch and turn on the light, which floods the room, unveiling all its beauty.

Jason and I had chosen the best accommodation money could buy, wanting our first night as man and wife to be extra special – something we could look back on and treasure.

My pupils contract trying to get adjusted to the bright light, causing me to blink a few times. The suite is magnificent, with a huge king-size bed in the center, surrounded by exquisite furnishings and expensive paintings adorning the walls.

Finally, I can take off the darn heavy wedding gown which has been like a burden all night. Dear me, most women fantasize about wearing these gowns but have no idea how heavy and uncomfortable they are.

Slowly, I undo the zipper, allowing the dress to fall to the floor. Exhausted, I flop on the bed in my undies, hoping Jason doesn't stay too long at the reception and joins me soon. This is our wedding night after all, and despite the shortcomings of our relationship during the past few weeks, I think a good bout of marital sex is just what the doctor ordered to cheer up my shoddy spirit.

Being locked away in the sanctuary of the honeymoon suite with my husband soon to join me, calms my nerves, and slowly dispels my fears. Whatever Joey may have heard and I'm sure he meant well, was just not true. Jason is a good man and we will live happily ever after.

Rising out of bed, I shed the rest of my clothes, and strolling into the bathroom turn on the shower handle, and allow the warm water to soak away my anxiety.

Now I feel cleansed and invigorated.

Turning off the golden faucet, I step out of the shower and grab a towel, taking care to dry every inch of my body. My reflection in the mirror tells me

I still have an amazing body...thick and curvy body which for some reason men have always adored. I love the way I look and never had any hang-ups about not being model-thin. For me, big is beautiful... much more of me for my husband to sample for the first time.

Yes, I am still a virgin. Jason had wanted to have sex, but I told him to save it for our wedding night. I guess that's why I allowed him to rush the wedding this fast so that he could claim my body, but in the sanctity of wedlock.

Stepping back into the bedroom, I'm ready to burst out in song, when a big, strong hand closes over my mouth, while an arm the size of a tree trunk grabs me around the waist, rendering me immobile. I struggle with my assailant and try to scream for help, but to no avail. The man is as strong as an ox and I am powerless in his grasp.

"Shhh...do not try and scream or I will snap your neck like a twig," A gruff voice orders. It's one of those voices that you know you would disobey at your own peril, so I slowly nod my head.

Morbid thoughts are pinging back and forth in my brain. All this feels like a terrible nightmare.

Joey was right.

I'm about to be murdered.

Cold terror grips me in its icy embrace. I say

a silent prayer. *Lord, I'm just a young woman. I don't want to die like this. Please spare me and I promise I will be a good* girl.

"I will take my hands from your mouth if you promise not to scream, Khloe. If you scream you are a dead woman," the voice of doom proclaims.

Again, I nod my head. I can do nothing but watch, paralyzed with fright.

My assailant slowly spins me around, still holding me by the waist and I gaze into a pair of the most gorgeous blue eyes I have ever seen in my life. There is a softness about them, though, not the look you would imagine of a hardened, cold-blooded killer.

He is looking at me, brows furrowed with a curious expression on his face, as if not sure what to make of me. *So is this really what a hitman looks like?*

His eyes stray toward my chest and only then do I remember I'm still draped in my towel. A blush sweeps across my face. I don't know why I am blushing in front of a man who is about to take my life.

Trying to breathe calmly so as not to upset the man, my gaze settles on his face and I detect thick defined eyebrows, an angular nose, dimpled cheeks, and a jawline so sharp it could cut diamonds. The man is ruggedly handsome and if you should clean him, he could pass for a fashion model; a far cry from what I imagined a killer would look like. He looks like he belongs on a spread in *Vogue* magazine.

His face is, however, the total opposite of what else I am seeing before me. The rest of his body is powerful…and I mean Herculean powerful. He is Trump Towers tall, with massive arms and biceps closer to the size of my waist; his chest bulging almost to his face.

What a freaking hunk. This man can't be a killer. Someone is playing a wedding joke on me.

"So …you are the one my husband hired to kill me?" I stutter, my heart in my mouth.

A puzzled expression creases his decadently fetching face. "How did you know that?" He huffs a breath, blue eyes widening.

My heart has leaped into my mouth but I remember a friend telling me that if I was ever in physical danger, that I should try and talk to my assailant so they can see me as a person. "Someone told me to run or my husband would have me killed tonight."

"So why didn't you?" His tone is harsh and for some reason, his breaths are coming out in short, sharp pants like the opening gusts of a hurricane.

"Didn't I what?"

"Run… like the person told you to?"

"It was just before the wedding and I had nowhere to escape." My chest heaves and for some reason, it is becoming quite unnerving being so close to this man and it's not because he is about to be my executioner. "And besides where would I go. I have nowhere to hide – all my immediate family members are dead."

His eyes seem to soften even more, changing from the dark blue of the deep sea to a more angelic blue. Suddenly, he pulls me closer to him until I can smell his overpoweringly masculine scent. "This may sound funny coming from me, but I'm really sorry." His voice is almost a whisper, his hot breath brushing against my cheeks.

So this is it. This is the end. I'm about to experience what death feels like. This is more than a fright, it is a freezing of the soul.

Lord, I'm only twenty-one. I don't want to die.

Chapter 5

Whit

Seeing her standing there, like a delicate flower; still in her wedding gown, somewhere between frightened and resigned, I know I can't do it.

I can't kill this beautiful, frail creature, whose only crime is that of marrying a heartless bastard. Her husband, who should be her protector, has thrown her to the wolves, expecting to benefit from her demise.

It won't happen tonight, Jason Gray. I just can't take her life.

My heartbeat threatens to break open my chest as Khloe takes off her wedding dress and stands there in nothing but red, see-through underwear.

From my vantage point behind the drapes, I can feel my cock begin to harden until it becomes a fucking tent pole in my pants

Khloe's body is one word – magnificent. This is the kind of body over which wars were fought and for which warriors would do battle to claim as the prize.

She is voluptuous beyond belief. Her breasts proudly jut out like small, ripe melons; her sides flow to a tiny waist that my arm can easily encircle; flaring out into large, curvy hips and a round ass that makes my mouth go fucking dry. My mind is flush with thoughts of having her bent over while I pump her from behind and feel the cheeks of that bountiful ass slapping against my balls.

I am transfixed in my hiding place and I can't stop staring at her magnificent face and per-fect body. This fucking plus-size goddess of desire is causing my balls to fill up and if she touches that sweet pussy I am going to nut in my pants

For a fleeting moment, my imagination wan-ders....to the image of myself licking into her mouth, drinking of her nectar...my tongue explor-ing every inch of her curvy body, stopping at those melons and sucking them until she is panting... and wanting more.

In my mind's eye, I see my tongue licking her clit while my fingers grip her nipples...lapping up the love juices flowing from her buffed pussy. My tongue snaking its way inside her, as she wraps her bountiful thighs around my neck, pulling me in deeper.

My cock throbs in anticipation of pumping her tender flesh….of fucking her hard and fast, sending her into orbit…flooding her insides with my seed.

I have to catch myself from letting out a growl and I moan inward brokenly. *How the fuck can I kill a woman like this?* Just when it appeared all the goodness had vanished from my sorry soul, a small sliver has raised its head.

Ever since I became a Hitman, shortly after leaving Navy Seal Team Bravo, I have had a creed never to kill a child and also shied away from killing women wherever possible.

No, no…no way. This is one contract I have to abort.

Khloe flops on the bed for a few minutes, before getting up and heading toward the bathroom. Soon, I hear her splashing in the shower so I hurry from my hiding place and plant myself behind the bathroom door.

My first order of business is to stop her from screaming. I'm sure she has no idea what's in store for her, but women like to scream their silly heads off at the slightest sign of danger.

Eventually, she exits the bathroom, and

emerging from my hiding place I quickly cover her mouth with one hand, and grab her waist with the other, pulling her into me. Her nubile frame shivers in fear against my hard body, causing my pulse to race in Usain Bolt-like fashion.

Khloe... you feel so damn good.

It takes a while for her to stop struggling and trying to scream...only then do I instruct her to be quiet.

As I turn her around, our eyes meet. There is a look of fear, yet acceptance in her eyes, and then she asks if I am the one her husband sent to kill her.

How did she know? What the heck is going on here?

The fear in her eyes is now replaced by one of sadness...curiosity even. "I know you have to do your job and kill me, but can I talk to you just a little first...if you don't mind?" she pleads, in that soft, girlish voice of hers. I know what she is trying to do and if it were anyone else, they would be dead right now.

I glare at her. "Yes, I do mind...I don't like to talk to someone I am about to kill."

But talk she does, anyway. "You don't look like a killer?" Khloe blurts out.

I know she is trying to use reverse psychology

on me, but I humor her anyway. "What does a killer look like?"

"You know… creepy-looking guys with scars on their cheeks, broken teeth, and shifty eyes." Her eyes are wet and wild.

Despite the tenseness of the situation I can't help but crack a smile. There is just something naïve and innocent about this goddess that keeps taking my breath away. "That's just what you see in the movies…in real life, anyone could be an assassin… even a woman like you."

Her eyes rake me up and down. "But you look like a model," she blurts out, gnawing at her bottom lip, pink tongue darting from side-to-side

"No, I don't," I cackle. "I am an ugly bastard both inside and out, and don't you forget it."

"Why did he pay you to kill me?" Her tone suddenly changes to one of angst.

If this woman is an actress, she is good…darn good. "It's not my job to ask questions, just carry out the task that I am paid to do."

"Don't you ever want to know?"

"No, I don't. Curiosity killed the cat."

Her nostrils flare and eyes narrow, "Did I come cheap?" That question knocks me out of my comfort zone. I never saw that one coming.

"No." I squint. "You were very expensive."

"Listen…whatever your name is." Khloe's fears seem to have been replaced by her more practical side. "My dad died and left me a fortune, so I'm a very wealthy woman. I can double whatever they paid you to kill me…just let me go, please."

"I have code," I whisper to her, my eyes somehow betraying me by flirting with hers. "If I renege on a job, I'm finished. No one would ever hire me again. And in this business reputation is everything."

I can't seem to stop her from talking. "I'm just a young woman. I don't want to die. I have my entire life to live. Can't you break your code, just this once?" Khloe stares at me, liquid flashing behind her eyelids, as if she is looking at a man she is out on a date with, not the man hired to kill her.

Despite our strange meeting I somehow sense a connection. There is something about her that I'm somehow incapable of ignoring. "You're a very interesting young woman, Khloe." My bold eyes rake her soft skin. "Unlike any woman I have ever met before…and believe me, I have met a lot."

She furrows her brow and gazes at me helplessly through tear-tipped lashes. "So you're a player as well as a hitman, hmm."

Despite myself, I crack a smile. His girl is

something else. "Not my fault that women seem to find me attractive."

"God, you are so full of yourself." Khloe rolls her eyes at me. "Just because you have a great body and model looks, now you think you are God's gift to women."

"So you have been noticing my body?" I ask. Khloe blushes, lowering her eyes. She swallows a lump in her throat and fidgets slightly, as if caught off-guard by my question.

Then a curious thing happens. She finally stops talking and closes her eyes. "I am ready. Go ahead and do what you came to do. Just tell me one thing first."

Her acquiescence comes as a complete surprise. "What's that?" My voice is strained.

"Tell me your name," she says in that melodic voice that is beginning to tug at my heartstrings.

I hesitate a second. "My name…." I take a deep breath. "They call me Whit."

Khloe sucks in air and her shoulder goes rigid. "Okay, Whit…please do it quickly so that it doesn't hurt." Her voice is trembling now and her body quivering against mine.

She has accepted her fate.

Looking at the gorgeous, fragile woman in

front of me, I know I can't go through with it. "I won't kill you Khloe, but you have to come with me, or we are both dead...do you understand?"

Her eyes open wide in disbelief and she shyly nods her head. Her breathing is harsh and fear shines in her eyes like a volcano exploding.

I pick her up in my arms, pull a robe over her to hide her semi-nude body, and carry her out of the room. My gun is in my hand, ready to take down anyone who tries to stop me from saving her.

There is no backing out now either. I have to take her with me.

Yes, I may have just signed my death sentence. I know her mobster husband will stop at nothing to kill us both.

As we ride the elevator to the ground floor, I keep my eyes peeled praying no one else has pressed the buttons. My gun is at the ready, knowing that these guys sometimes hire back-up in case a job goes south. But anyone who tries to stop me tonight will face my wrath.

The coast is clear and we exit the back entrance and run toward my car parked in the alley behind the hotel. Pushing Khloe down in the back seat, I gun the engine to life and roar off down the street. From her vantage point in the back, I feel her eyes on me, so I turn around. Her eyes are filled with tears of gratitude.

Don't thank me just yet, baby, we still have a treacherous road ahead.

"You can relax and rest now Khloe…it's a long ride."

She doesn't even ask me where we are going, the gleam in her eyes is enough…for now.

Chapter 6

Khloe

He thinks I'm asleep, but I'm only pretending. I catch him staring at me several times. There is a tenderness hidden deep inside those cold, dark eyes that you would never expect from a cold-blooded killer like Whit.

Even now, I have no idea why he saved me. It would have been easy for him to just kill me in the hotel suite, make it look like an accident, and collect all the blood money my scum of a husband intended to pay.

Tears start to well in my eyes, but I force them back. *This is not the time to cry, Khloe. You have to be strong.*

I finally stir and open my eyes, peering from the back seat at Whit behind the wheel, still in disbelief at the way he looks. He is a gorgeous man, nothing like what you would expect a killer to be. His face is almost angelic and his body, oh my goodness… tall and powerful, with arms almost the size of my waist.

When he accosted me in the honeymoon suite I just couldn't believe that someone who looked like him could be so evil; a paid murderer.

I'm not fooling myself though. Yes, he may have saved me, but for what selfish reason? Maybe he wants me for himself. To hold me captive and have his way with me sexually, before killing me and discarding the evidence.

A chill runs through my body at the thought of being Whit's sex slave. At the same time though, a perverse thrill causes my heart to flutter inside my chest. Somehow the thought of being assaulted by Whit doesn't seem as repulsive to me as it should.

Snap out of it, Khloe…this man is a paid killer. Don't be fooled by his choir boy looks.

The uncanny thing about what has transpired tonight is that somewhere during all the drama, a strange connection seems to have developed between both of us. Something happened in the penthouse suite which I still can't fathom. When we looked at each other, tension had filled the atmosphere…one that you could cut with a knife.

It was as if Whit had cast a spell over me. I wouldn't scream, even if I could. And when his massive hands closed around my neck, he froze. He couldn't squeeze the life out of my body.

Even now, when I look at him, butterflies seem to float around in the region of my tummy, and my pulse skitters for some reason.

"So you're awake." Whit's voice booms in my ears, piercing the stillness of the night and brings me back to reality. It's dark outside so I have no idea where we are heading.

"Where...where are you taking me?" I hear myself stammer.

His eyes are following me in the rearview mirror. "Somewhere safe for now," he answers gruffly. "Don't worry, you're safe with me." He repeats the line as if to reassure not just me, but himself as well.

Attempting to stretch the tension out of my body, I squirm around in my seat, digging my toes into the flooring, while looking for recognizable landmarks.

"I have a few safe houses stashed around New York that we can hide out in because I don't want to hit the highways just yet, it will be too easy for them to track us down." Whit glances over at me for a second and I shiver at the sight of his dark, brooding eyes. "By now your hubby would have realized I took you, but what he won't know is why so that gives us a chance to come up with a game plan."

"Thanks, I guess," I mutter under my breath.

"You are welcome, Khloe." The man has super sensitive ears. I had no idea he had even heard me.

The Manhattan skyline recedes and I realize we are heading towards Brooklyn. "My husband…" I know it's not the time for talking and Whit seems deep in this own thoughts, but I have to know. "Why would he want to have me killed?"

"You gotta be kidding me?" Whit huffs, managing to keep his eyes on the road and others vehicle whiz pass.

"No…I really don't know," I say honestly. "This is all very puzzling to me."

Whit dims his bright headlights and stretches his broad frame. "The money girl. For these mob guys, it's always about the money."

My stomach churns and I almost vomit. "Mob?" I rasp. "What are you saying; that Jason is involved with the Mafia? I don't believe it."

Whit glances over his shoulder at me. "You had no idea, did you?"

I am wide awake now, adrenalin course through my veins. "You mean he deliberately married me just for the money he would get after having me killed? Oh, my God." My fingers grip the back of Whit's seat and I hold my head down. My chest is tight. I am having trouble breathing.

He grunts and glances over his shoulder at me. "Grow up girl; people are killed for a lot less than what you inherited…a lot less."

Slumping in my seat, my mind wanders back to the times I spent with Jason, and I start picking up on the little warning signals I had been too blind to see, or maybe in my grief and need for a knight in shining armor, just didn't want to see.

"I don't mean to be a bother, Whit, but tell me one more thing…who really is my husband? Who is Jason Gray?" I now realize I know nothing about this man, or what I thought I knew is all turning out to be a lie.

Whit takes a deep breath, slams his foot down on the pedal, seemingly in anger. The car picks up speed. "Your dear husband is highly connected to the mob. He is one of their partners in New York, with ties to you name it…drugs, prostitution, and gambling. That's one sick son-of-a-bitch you just got yourself hitched up with, girl."

My mind goes numb and my body collapses helplessly. Feelings of shame, guilt, and remorse snake through my body. To say I'm shocked out of my wits is putting it mildly.

Closing my eyes for a minute, I begin pondering how the heck my real estate developer dad would know someone as devious and dangerous as Jason. Maybe he hadn't known who he really was.

There are more questions than answers flooding my mind, and I look over at Whit, searching for clues. "I know there are lots you want to know, girl, but for now let's just get you to safety until I figure out our next move."

I nod my head, sighing audibly. "There's just one more thing, Whit."

"Yes, little girl. What's that?"

My head bobs in an annoyed manner. "Stop calling me girl," I speak briskly. "I am twenty-one years old and you make me feel like I'm a baby. Please call me by my name. It's Khloe, okay."

He laughs out loud for the first time since we met. No, not a laugh, more like a bellow, or a howl, and I can't help but be swept up in his contagious joy and I find myself laughing along. "You're a pretty cheeky one, aren't you, Khloe," Whit chirps, after finally bringing himself to stop laughing.

My arms fold across my chest defiantly. "I'm not the little girl you think I am," I huff. "I may have lived a sheltered life, but I'm very smart, I'll have you know." I lean over and bat my lashes at him and he laughs again, causing my eyes to rest on his lips, noticing the way they part and his tongue slithers along its velvet-like surface.

Whit is a damn sexy man, no two ways about it.

Chapter 7

Whit

I pull up into a warehouse in Brooklyn and press the buzzer to open the garage gate before driving inside. "Come on Khloe, get your pretty little ass out of the car. This is where we going to stay tonight," I say in a playful tone, my mood lightened by our recent byplay in the car.

"This is a strange place for an apartment. Where are we going to sleep?" Khloe blurts out, her eyes scanning the empty warehouse where two other cars and some machinery are scattered about.

"There is a bedroom, living room, and bathroom in the back," I say mockingly, starting to empty the car.

"Oh...just one room?" Khloe makes a face.

I resist the urge to slap her on the ass. "Khloe, for god's sake, I'll sleep in the living room...on the couch." My eyes widen in disbelief. "I'm not that kinda guy…I kill, I don't rape."

"That's not what I was thinking," she blushes, caught with her pants down.

That's exactly what you were thinking.

I pop the trunk and remove my bag filled with two automatics and a few cell phones. I like to travel light, just in case I'm ever stopped by the cops for some silly, routine traffic violation. The rest of my hardware is hidden in my personal apartment, which I want to stay away from for now, just in case somebody made me.

We enter the sparsely, but tastefully decorated apartment in the back of the warehouse and I direct Khloe to the bedroom in which she will be sleeping. "But I don't have anything to change into or sleep in?" she protests.

Trust a woman to be thinking about stuff like that, when was it not for me she would now be lying face down, dead on a hotel bathroom floor. "Sleep in the clothes you are wearing just for tonight," I say gently. "Tomorrow, I'll go shopping and get you all the stuff you need. I didn't plan this part, remember."

Khloe bats her lashes gratefully. "You're right. What was I thinking, sorry Whit."

"Don't worry about it, babe….I mean Khloe." I smile as does she.

God, this girl is so damn gorgeous. I don't know how I'm going to survive this period around her. Just the sight of her makes me horny as hell.

Khloe heads toward the bedroom and in a few minutes, I hear the sound of running water.

Planting myself on the sofa in the living room, I glance through the slight opening in the bathroom door. I can make out her shadow against the wall.

My cock twitches, involuntarily. Damn, even her shadow has curves.

I check both my cell phones to see if I had missed any calls during all the excitement. There was none, so I turn the volumes back up and place them on the table beside me. Next, I retrieve the two guns from my bag and also put them down on the table. My trusted personal firearm stays in my shoulder holster, just where I like it.

Khloe switches off the light and then sticks her beautiful neck through the door. "Good night, Whit," she coos, brown eyes twinkling with what I figure to be gratitude.

I feel fucking achy all over. "Good night, Khloe. Sleep tight. Don't let the bed bugs bite."

She looks at me with a curious expression on her face. "I know I have been a bitch, but thanks for all you have done. Whit, thanks for sparing my life."

She crinkles her brow before shutting the door.

After hearing her words of gratitude, I'm happier than ever that I spared her life. Fuck, this is the one decent thing I have done in a long time and if anyone deserves that moment of weakness I showed, it's Khloe.

My watch says midnight. It's going to be a long, sleepless night for me. No way will I take a chance and nod off, not until I hit up my contacts and hear what the buzz is on the grapevine. The one advantage I have in my favor is that they won't know why I took her. They'll probably figure it's for ransom or some shit, which will give me a couple of days to plan my next move because as of right now I haven't the slightest clue what that move will be.

I'm halfway into my nocturnal vigil when Khloe's scream pierces the stillness of the night.

Shit...what is it now?

I grab my gun and burst into her room, ready to cut down any intruder, but there's no one around, just Khloe sitting up in bed sobbing, shaking like a leaf.

"What the matter?" I run over toward the bed and plant my ass beside her.

"I had a nightmare, Whit," she sobs, chest jerking up and down. "I dreamt I was dead."

The way her fucking tits juggle under her blouse has me groaning inwardly. "It was just a dream," I assure her. "It's natural after all you have been through to have dreams like that, trust me."

Khloe hugs me tightly, leaning her head against my chest, still sobbing. I cradle her in my arms, feeling her heart wracking against mine and her tears streaming down my chest.

I deliberately cling to her for a while, not wanting to lose the incredible feeling of her nubile body against mine...her tender flesh causing electric currents to spark between us. And then I realize that Khloe is only wearing panties under the covers and her firm breasts are sticking into my chest, causing my cock to stir.

Shit, I slowly pull away. There is no way she can't feel the erect monster throbbing between my legs. Yes, it's a big cock, or so I have been told.

Khloe finally lies back down, pulling the sheet over her naked body, but her hand tugs at my leg. "Don't leave yet, just sit here until I fall asleep, please?" She pleads with her eyes. My cock is swelling at an alarming rate and my breathing is becoming labored. Pre-cum is dribbling out of the head of my shaft and the white juice is filling up my balls real fast. I can't help it, my eyes peek at her tits and I am broken. Heat is churning in my belly. These are breasts made to drive a man to sin.

"I promise I'll stay." I grin reassuringly, again observing her large breasts against the thin fabric of the sheets...my eyes scanning the outline of her sexy, lace honeymoon panties, even in the dim light.

I'm horny as hell. I need to fuck, and if not her then I need to fuck someone, but I know I can't leave Khloe alone in the warehouse in the vulnerable condition she is in.

Eventually, she falls asleep, but the throbbing between my legs remains. Walking back into the living room and grabbing my cellphone, I punch in some digits I haven't dialed in a long time.

"Whit, is that you?" A sexy, familiar voice from the past coos on the other end of the line.

"Yes, Camille...it's me."

"You son-of-a-bitch, it's been over a year, why haven't you called me?"

"Been on jobs all over the country...you know how it is being a traveling salesman," I remark, referring to the cover I use as my alter ego.

"Why are you calling at this hour, you know I like my beauty sleep?"

"I'm horny and I want to fuck you."

"Just like that?"

"Yes, just like that."

There is silence on the line. Camille Montana is an advertising executive by day and super freak by night. We had met a year earlier at a club and fucked each other silly for a few days before I had to leave on a job. Camille likes a strong man; one who dominates her. She is a take-charge bitch at work, so sexually she likes to be submissive and let a man have the upper hand.

"Damn you, Whit. I would love to come over and fuck your brains out for old time's sake, but I have company tonight, so I can't make it."

Dammit, what's a man to do when his prick's the size of a watermelon, and there is an ache for the goddess sleeping in the room next door?

It's been ages since I have spanked my monkey, but tonight I need release. Closing my eyes, I whip out my cock, gently stroking it as I begin my fantasy about Khloe.

Closing my eyes, I imagine her opening the bedroom door slowly walking over to me, naked, her breasts quivering, hips flaring and perfect, long legs striding forward.

I imagine pulling her down into the sofa beside me, my lips seeking hers urgently and I kiss her passionately. Her lips taste like a fresh spring morning and she moans as my tongue snakes into her mouth.

It seems so real, me tweaking her nipples, causing her to shiver and her already hard tits become even more swollen. I circle each nipple with my lips as she moans and reaches for my cock, encircling the head with her fingers, sending a jolt of electricity throughout my body.

My tongue slithers down her perfect tummy, while I caress her ass...man that ass, jutting out like the bottom of a Coca-Cola bottle. Perfect...almost too perfect. Her body convulses as I run my tongue along the folds of her sweet pussy and my fingers trail down her crack.

"Whit." I imagine hearing her moan loudly. "Oh God, Whit your tongue feels so good on my pussy."

My cock is on fire, it needs to be sucked.

"Lick it," I say, issuing an order, not a request.

"It's so big..." There is a scared look in her eyes.

"Suck it now," I command, my tone ominous.

I imagine Khloe dropping to her knees and gently licking the head of my cock, which quivers at her touch. Emboldened, she continues licking like she is slurping on a lollypop. Man alive, it feels so good and it takes all my willpower not to cum on her lips.

Khloe's luscious mouth slowly descends on my prick and she sucks on the head, while I ever so gently fuck her mouth. The sight of her gorgeous face kneeling in front of me while she sucks me off only serves to heighten my pleasure. Heat settles in my groin and I am mad with desire and animal longing.

It's all too much for me, so grabbing the back of Khloe's head, I pull her up toward me. "I have to fuck you now," I say gruffly, carnality flooding my voice.

Khloe slips onto my lap and I gently guide the head of my cock inside her now wet and quivering pussy. Fuck, she is tight, and at first my cock can't go in, but soon it slides inside and I start pumping her slowly, my hands on her hips controlling the action. This woman has the tightest pussy I have had the privilege of entering and when she grinds those perfect hips, I am lost. Khloe starts rotating her hips more urgently and I know she is about to cum.

"Whit...Whit... my god, this is the best fuck ever..." In my head, her voice trails off into a scream and she thrashes around on my dick like a fish caught on a hook.

"Oh my god. Just don't stop, just fuck me, stud." I imagine her continuing to moan, her pussy clenching, milking my cock. I hang on for dear life as

I feel my orgasm building up and with a sharp jolt of my hips I flood her insides, grabbing into her hips to keep myself from ramming into her and hurting her with my shaft.

I open my eyes, but there is no Khloe, just the sight of my semen splattering the floor in front of me. What a fucking fantasy. It's now fully dawning on me that this captive of mine is going to drive me freaking crazy with lust.

How can I keep myself from tasting and pumping that sweet tender pussy?

Chapter 8

Khloe

I have a burning need to pee which disturbs my sleep. Jumping up, I rush to the bathroom to relieve myself, before heading back to bed. Somehow, with Whit around, I feel safe. Well as safe as a girl can feel when she is on the run from her killer of a husband.

The bedroom door is slightly ajar and I'm about to spring back into bed when a rustle outside grabs my attention. Not wanting to disturb Whit in case he is asleep, I gently tiptoe toward the door and peer through the opening. The living room is dark save for the light from a small lamp in the corner. My eyes scan the room from my vantage point and I make out Whit sitting on the couch, eyes closed, and massive prick in his hand, pumping away.

What the heck? My mouth opens and my cheeks flush. The hitman is furiously fisting his dick

I try to look away, but I can't. It's the biggest

dick I have ever seen in my life, not that I've seen many. I know I should feel embarrassed, but somehow the sight of this gorgeous man masturbating sends a shiver throughout my body and I feel an unfamiliar trickling between my thighs.

I'm feeling all swoony and achy all over. The flesh between my thighs is agitated and a gasp escapes my lips

My panties are flooding. Instinctively my fingers reach between my legs and I slowly massage my clit. My breath spills out in torrents as I watch Whit feverishly stroking his tool and I find myself imagining it inside me…filling me up. I imagine his hard powerful body on top of mine, his prick slamming into me and I have to place a hand over my mouth to keep from screaming.

Then I feel a quivering in my loins which tells me I am about to have an orgasm.

So quickly? How can this be?

I have never had a real, earth-shattering orgasm like the ones I read about in romance books. Even when I have used my fingers to try and quench my desires, it had been very difficult making myself cum. I stroke my clit feverishly the faster Whit pumps his dick until I feel a tsunami explode between my legs, almost causing me to topple over.

It takes all the willpower I can muster to stop myself from screaming at the sight of Whit semen exploding from his dick, and on weakened legs, I slowly make my way back to bed and crawl under the sheets.

What's happening to me? Just twenty-four hours ago this man was a stranger and now he has me weak in the knees and stirs up an ache between my legs with the slightest glance.

I will have to be very careful around Whit, he is a dangerous man, not just with guns, but also that mighty cannon between his legs.

***

I awake to the familiar aroma of bacon and eggs filling the room. Jumping out of bed, I quickly dash into the shower to wash away any remnant of my masturbation a few hours ago. We had left the hotel so quickly, that I hadn't even had time to pack a makeup kit, so all I can do for now is slick back my hair and straighten my brows with my fingers.

Ugh, I think I look horrible in the mornings. Then it dawns on me that I actually want to look good for Whit.

Cautiously, I open the door and tiptoe outside in an effort to investigate where the mouth-watering smell is emanating from. There is a kitchen adjoining the living room and I peer inside to see none other than Whit making breakfast. "How do you like your eggs?" he asks matter-of-factly as if it were the most natural thing in the world to be preparing breakfast for the woman he was sent to murder.

I am shocked. "So you…cook too?" The words hitch in my throat.

"Of course Khloe," he says briskly. "A guy like me has to know how to look after himself, even though I don't normally keep women around for breakfast," Whit responds with a wink, a smile creasing his devastatingly handsome face.

"I guess so." There is a tremor in my voice. "But where did you learn to cook?"

"Funny enough, in the army of all places." He turns over a crispy slice of bacon and the worms in my tummy jump in glee.
"I was always getting into trouble and my commanding officers would assign me to help out in the mess hall as punishment, knowing how I hated to cook." There is a twinkle in his eyes as he reminisces.

"I like my eggs medium well," I say, taking a seat at the small dining table. The place has a masculine feel about it, but it's clean and presentable.

"Shh, no more questions until I'm finished," Whit announces, just as I'm about to open my mouth. So I smile and watch him carefully place the eggs and bacon and orange juice in front of me. "We will lay low for a few days, so you will have to tell me what you like and I will go shopping." He rolls his eyes. "You can't leave the warehouse just yet, since by now I'm sure you are probably the most pursued woman in the country."

My burrows furrow and I rest my elbows on the table. "What do you mean?"

He blows a harsh breath and takes a seat in front of me. A condescending smirk is daubed all over his face. "I mean, by now your husband would have had to call in the police and the mob will also be searching for us."

This is all too much for me to fathom, so I just settle on enjoying my breakfast. "This is so tasty, Whit," I remark between mouthfuls. "You have to cook for me again."

He merely laughs and wolfs down his sausage, downing it with a pint of beer. "Beer for breakfast?" I kick his foot under the table.

"Didn't sleep last night and beer keeps me going and going." He smiles, killing me with his pearly white teeth and perfect facial structure. *I bet you didn't sleep, after all, you were playing with that big dick all night.*

Finally, we both finish eating and Whit settles back in his chair and stares at me. My eyes remain lowered, unable to match his intense scrutiny. "So what's our game plan?" I finally find my voice, my fingers drumming on the table as if having a life of their own.

"We are going to have to transform you into someone that no one will ever recognize." He chuckles as if amused by my debacle. "I'm going out to buy some hair dye, scissors, clothes, and make-up for you."

"Okay..." Is all I can say, my mind floating all over the place.

Whit presses his palm firmly together. "Not that that will be easy." His blue eyes have darkened. "Since you are one of the most beautiful women in the world and people will notice you wherever we go, no matter how you look."

I blush like crazy and my nipples become painful as they stiffen. Warning sirens are blaring in my head. *So he really thinks I am beautiful, wow.*

I don't know why, but it matters to me what this man thinks and I feel goosebumps prickling my skin. "Then, we are going downstairs into the sound-proof shooting gallery, so I can teach you how to fire a gun," Whit says. "As of now, you have to start learning how to defend yourself, just in case it's needed."

"I fire a gun?" I blurt out in disbelief. "I don't even like being around guns."

His palms slam on the table. "This time it could be a matter of life or death." Whit rises from the table and paces the room like a caged tiger.

I get up, ready to follow him, but he turns around and waves his massive hands at me. "You know that you are the one washing up the dishes, right?" He chuckles, wiggling his nose teasingly.

Despite my misgivings, I am relishing the task of making myself useful, rather than just feeling like a sitting duck. I immediately attend to my assigned task, finishing the plates and frying pan in a jiffy, and join Whit in the living room where his eyes are glued to the television set.

As he had predicted, I made the morning news. Each station leads with a story of the heiress who disappeared on her wedding night, posting photos and calling on the public to assist in locating me. "Now, you see why we have to change the way you look?" He says in a serious tone. Gone is the kidding around and he is suddenly all business.

I nod my head and flop into the couch.

Whit is heading to the bathroom when he turns. "There's only one bathroom here, so I hope you don't mind me showering."

"Not at all," I chirp, shaking my head. "Just don't leave the toilet seat up." Whit begins laughing so hard and I join in, enjoying the moment of relief. These are precious moments of gaiety and I will take them when I can.

Ten minutes later Whit is back in the living

room. He is sporting a pair of jeans that shows off his muscled thighs. His hair is damp and slicked back, and I can't help but look on admiringly. Everything about this man is gorgeous.

There is a fire raging in the juncture between my thighs and a fire in my belly at the thought of him and his exposed monster dick last night. *Why am I feeling this way? What is happening to me?*

"I have to run out for a while." Whit looks me squarely in the eyes. "I'll lock the door behind me and you open for no one, you hear, not even me."

The menacing look on his face makes me realize how scary he can be. "It's for your sake. Trust me Khloe, these guys don't want you back alive...they would rather kill you first."

My body shudders at his words, knowing I'm caught in a no-win situation. For some reason, however, I trust him. With him around, I feel safe and secure. *Whit will protect me. He won't allow anyone to harm me.*

He pats me on the shoulder and exits the room. I hear the key turning and grills being locked. This is indeed a safe house; no way is anyone getting in through that entrance.

After he departs, I notice the gun lying on the side table; not that I know how to use it, but despite my reservations about guns, I would sure as hell try if anyone tries to harm me.

I return to watching the news. Only God knows how I going to get out of this situation.

Chapter 9

Whit

The world of a hitman is shrouded in mystery. You stay alive by remaining a ghost, a malevolent phantom who blends in the shadow and goes around without anyone noticing you.

I have remained alive and above the law, because no one knows who I am. But I'm not a fool. I know my cover could be blown at any time, so I have several aliases that I rotate. I also have several safe houses in and out of New York. I never leave anything to chance.

So I drive around for a few blocks, making sure I'm not being followed, before stopping at a nondescript beauty store. Parking discreetly, I put on a cap and dark glasses and saunter inside. The pretty young cashier smiles as she looks up at me. I smile back, being careful to avoid the camera, and set about picking up the products I need. Khloe would stand out too much if I dyed her hair blonde, so I settle on making her into a redhead. I also purchase her makeup and other feminine products.

I pay the cashier, who gives me another toothy smile, and then I proceed to make several stops at clothing stores and the supermarket before heading back to the safe house.

It's a relieved-looking Khloe who greets me upon my return. "Whit, I have never been so happy to see anyone in my life," she blurts out, giving me a big hug which catches me off guard.

"You don't have to worry about me girl, no one messes with Whit," I say defiantly.

Khloe grabs the bags from my hands, like a typical woman, excited at the prospect of trying on new clothes. She carefully examines the items, making a face, or smiling, depending on what strikes her fancy.

She finally looks up at me. "Not too bad, for a man."

"You gave me great sizes." I laugh and warmth spreads in my tummy. "So let's get right to work. We are going to cut your hair then color it."

"That I can do." Khloe beams, her eyes sparkling like polished South African diamonds. "I'm pretty good with hair and makeup, so just let me do my thing."

I feign offense. "Well excuse me, miss hair-stylist," I say, letting out a loud whistle as the muscles twitch in my cheek.

She lets out a hearty laugh and disappears into the bathroom.

Flopping into the couch, my immediate job is deciding which weapon I should use to test her with. I settle on the small automatic; that should suit her just fine.

I spend the next forty-five minutes flipping through the television channels before I hear footsteps and look up to see Khloe walking toward me. She is almost unrecognizable but just as beautiful. That's the one thing about her we can't change since no matter how different we make her look, she remains a showstopper.

"Damn," I exhale loudly, my eyes drinking in her unrivaled beauty. "You are just as gorgeous as a redhead."

Khloe laughs under her breath. "You really think so, Whit?".

"Yes, for sure no one will recognize you...not even me, damn." Khloe flashes her million-dollar smile and my entire world lights up. Something about this woman takes my breath away. Around her, you can't help but be sucked in by her beauty and charm. "Now it's time to teach you how to defend yourself and fire a gun in the event of an emergency." I get down to business, opening a door that leads downstairs to the basement. Khloe follows obediently.

I flick the light switch and hear her gasp as she surveys the room. It's a big place, with a target in the center of the room and several guns hanging on the wall and in corners. "Welcome to my practice room," I announce. "Don't worry, I have silencers and it's soundproof. No one will hear us down here."

A look of relief washes over her pretty face. "Come here," I order, planting her in front of me and placing the weapon in her hands. I hold her from behind, helping her curl her finger around the trigger. The feel of her body against mine sends a shock through my entire system. My heart feels as if it is punched by invisible objects and my cock strains against my jeans.

I want her naked and dripping in precious stones and my cum.

I'm losing it for this girl. She is fucking wrecking me.

***

Khloe and I spend the next three days cloaked away inside the warehouse, far away from the maddening crowd. During that time she learns how to shoot and after her initial reservations, turns out to be quite a willing student.

The more I place my arms around her while teaching her how to shoot, the more the sexual tension rises until these moments become a sort of byplay between us.

Her body fits snugly in my arms and her short, cropped hair makes her appear even sexier if that were possible. I'm starting to feel a familiar yearning between my legs. Her body in front of me is crying out for a man's touch. She is every man's sexual fancy and I am finding it hard to swallow when she is so close by.

Khloe's laughter is infectious, and despite the dilemma she has found herself in she never gets down on herself. She is indeed the most amazing woman I have ever met in my life.

On the third night, she is lying in bed watching movies, with me sitting beside her. Khloe is like that, she likes my company around her before she falls asleep. Her situation has rendered her afraid of the dark. "Whit," she says, a touch of shyness, or is it fear in her voice. "Tell me how you came about being the man you are today. How did you turn into a hitman?"

My eyes close for a minute and I exhale. I know I should tell her it's none of her business, after all, the less she knows about me the better her chance of survival. But hearing the pleading in her voice and her genuine desire for information, I decide to open up.

"For a while, I was a member of an elite Navy Seals squad. They taught me how to kill and I found out I was the best at it." I pause for a minute, memories flooding my consciousness. "When they booted me out of the squad for insubordination, I drifted for a few months, not sure what I wanted to do. The Seals had done its job well…killing was all I knew."

Khloe strains her ear, studying my face in that studious manner of hers. "Then a guy who I had known from the squad asked me to help him out with a job…taking out some gangbanger and paying me well to do it." My voice hardens. "It was easy money and I found out I enjoyed it, so I decided to learn the trade and then become a ghost, developing several aliases…a killer for hire that no one knew."

"Oh…" There is a tenderness in her voice, no make that compassion. And then it hits me square on the chops, like a phantom punch. I am falling irrevocably in love with Khloe Spencer. She has crept into uncharted territory of my feelings and claimed my heart. This strange, emotional feeling irks me greatly. Personal attachments are a weakness in my line of work.

"But you could have gotten out. Why not just leave?" She insists, bringing me back to reality.

"I didn't want to. I enjoy killing and most of

the people I killed deserved it anyway."

"What about a woman...wasn't there ever one to make you think twice about your chosen career?"

"Never, until..." I catch myself, almost letting the cat out of the bag.

'Until, what?" she pleads, eyes burning into my soul. Ears pricked as she holds her breath...waiting.

"Forget it." I look at her with a forlorn expression. I see the sparkle in her eyes; the way her lips tremble, and I know she is starting to feel the same way. Why else would she be so curious?

I want you, Khloe. I want to know you, to possess you, to fuck you silly. After you there can be no other. You have claimed my heart.

Chapter 10

Khloe

I am lying in bed listening to Whit tell me the story of how he became a hitman. It's a dark tale but at the same time a fascinating one.

Here is someone people would take for a cold-hearted killer and yet there is something warm and wonderful about him. Here is the man who risks his life for no reason to save me from certain death. He's a flawed hero, but nevertheless, my reluctant hero.

I coax him to tell me how he became the man he is today and as he admits his dark past, it becomes obvious...somehow, in this strange universe, the most unlikely thing is happening. I am falling in love with Whit. And to think I don't even know his last name, or if Whit is his real name.

The television drones on, but I have ceased watching; my eyes are glued to him, studying his masculine frame. Whit notices my stares and his eyes dart towards me. He licks his lips as he surveys my body. I'm dressed in a pair of shorts, a tube top, and my breasts protrude sharply.

Whit shifts uncomfortably as he relates his childhood and the unexpected loss of both parents in a car crash. Something inside me snaps. I want to hold him, comfort him, but instead, due to my shyness, all I can do is reach out and place my hands over his.

But this seems to be all the invitation Whit needs, as he kicks off his shoes and rolls over on the bed until he is right next to me, his eyes boring into mine; his hot breath oozing against my cheeks.

My heart beats precariously and my pulse skitters. My sex is clenching and I can feel the dampness in my crotch. Warmth swirls through my belly at the sight of him. I have never wanted a man as much as I want him at this moment.

Suddenly, without any warning, Whit touches my lips with a lustful finger, slowly tracing the delicate softness of my upper lip. I tremble in his arms as he cups my head and presses his lips against mine. My eyes become as round as saucers and I tense, but I can't resist, so my lips part and I kiss him back hungrily. The kiss is long and leisurely and a powerful force passes between us, a wild sensual heat.

"You sure, Khloe?" Whit's eyes plead.

"Yes," I whimper, shocked by my admission as

the words rush out of me. My heart is speeding out of control and a gasp fires from my throat. We kiss open-mouthed, tenderly at first then his lips become more demanding, cruel pieces of flesh that are devouring my will to resist.

Tension pools in my sex and electric currents spread to my finger and toes. I am meowing like a cat, greedy for the mild stored up in the sacs swinging between his legs.

Our lips lock for what seems like forever. His tongue forces its way into my mouth, seeking mine and together they wrestle for supremacy. "I wanted to fuck you from the first time I say you," Whit moans into my mouth. His filthy language makes me hit the ceiling.

My body is on fire, wetness trickling between my legs. I hear someone moaning until I realize it's me. "You turn me on like no other man ever has, Whit," I gurgle. "My body is crying out for your touch." I can't believe this woman is me. That I am pouring out my deepest feels to a man who is almost a complete stranger.

Finally, Whit removes his lips, but only to start kissing my neck and I nearly explode. His hot lips on my neck are driving me crazy, causing my body to convulse. A kiss like this can only have one conclusion. *But am I really ready for this?*

Whit's hands pull down my top and he

roughly cups my breasts. Fire explodes between my legs, as he tweaks my nipples and strokes them with his fingers. Then his magical tongue encircles my nipples and he sucks them gently, giving equal attention as if they are the most delicious pair in the world. How can I describe the feeling as juice sprays between my legs and I shudder over and over, lost in a sexual trance?

"Don't stop," I moan, writhing against the sheets. "Whit, please don't stop...I want this. Even if it just this one time, I need you inside me come what may."

His experienced hands loosen the buttons on my shorts and he quickly tugs them down my legs. His eyes are wild and his breathing uneven, like that of a wild beast.

Then every nerve goes crazy inside my already steaming body when he rips off my panties as if they were made of paper. His hands grip my ass cheeks, squeezing them and feeling satisfied at their firmness, he rubs his finger against my butt hole. "Shit," I squeal. "Whit, what are you doing?"

Whit simply ignores my outburst, clawing and raking his fingers into my innocent flesh. He slaps my butt and a heavy thrill runs up my spine.

In a flash, Whit whips off his clothes and is naked before me, pulling me into his arms. I can feel his big, hard dick rubbing against my tummy, the same dick I had seen a few nights ago. My hit-man looks at me and fists his cock, peeling back the fleshy covering and rolling it back in place. "Do you want me to stop?" he grunts and I can only shake my head.

He has a strange kind of magnetism that draws me to him. Whit's fingers begin exploring my body, slowly, then with more urgency and every inch of my body lights up with the urgent need to possess him. He parts my legs, stroking my folds and massaging my clit, the most sensitive organ on my body, which elicits a long, piercing howl that starts from my toes and winds its way to the top of my lungs. My sex is quivering and I feel pleasures in places I never knew existed.

I crumble and shatter as the ache between my legs becomes more insistent.

Whit opens my sex and slowly inserts one finger inside me, crooking it and massaging a flashy point that makes my body spill out a wet welcome to its intruder. "Holy shit..." I squeal, as I feel an orgasm tearing it way like a hurricane blasting across the open sea. "I am going to cum... baby, I am going to cum." But Whit does one better. Realizing my predicament, he dives between my legs and flutters his tongue on my clit, until I experience a little death. My legs close around his neck, pulling him in, while I grind my hips against his tongue. He sucks me raw, munching on my sex like a man who has not quenched his thirst in days.

"Ugh...Ugh," I wail over and over, my body shuddering as if in an epileptic fit. Whit frees himself from between my legs, grabs a condom from a drawer, and rolls it over his prick.

"It's too big," I babble nonsensically, wracked with pleasure. My eyes lock onto his dick which looks like it was fashioned out of iron.

"Don't worry, I will be gentle," he responds, in a voice filled with carnality.

Then in one motion, he places the head of his shaft between my legs. At first, it meets resistance, it can't go in.

"I'm a virgin, Whit," I finally disclose, staring into his eyes.

The look of surprise on his face tells his predicament. "Shit, are you for real," he blubbers. "But you had a fiancé?"

Biting my bottom lip, I try and draw him into me. "It's a long story but I wanted to wait until I was married," I purr.

"I don't know if my cock can fit inside a virgin."

"I want you to try," I moan. "I want you to be the first."

Whit sighs and slowly he pries the head of his monster shaft against the entrance to my treasure… easy…easy… He works it back and forth, moistening it in the juices cascading down my folds until the large mushroom of a head slips inside. "Fuck,: he grunts. "This is the tightest pussy I have ever had. Khloe, I am going to fuck you raw."

It hurts like crazy. I see stars, the moon, the sun, every freaking planet, as my life flashes before my eyes. "Yes, Whit," I sob. "I want you to sex me any way you want…I want you to pluck my cherry. I won't let him stop. Tonight I feel stretched and hot and no longer a girl, but a woman, a complete woman. If I don't make it through tomorrow, at least I will have the memory of tonight.

I feel the heat of Whit's dick forcing inside my virgin opening, slamming past my maidenhead. It hurts at first, then the hurt is replaced by a delicious, indescribable feeling, making me want more, of him…no, all of him. Grabbing his ass, I guide the rest of his prick inside until he is screwing me… gently… lovingly. Looking down I see my sex impaled on his shaft and delicious shudders pass through my core.

The sheet is stained with blood, proving that I am no longer innocent.

So this is what great sex is? Dear lord look what I have been missing.

My long legs clasp behind his back and Whit starts fucking me harder and deeper. "Sex me... screw me," I grunt, scream, moan, and call out his name, as he launches his assault. I never knew I had this is me, but which woman does until she is being pumped by a real man.

"This pussy is so good," Whit moans. "I never want my cock to come out of your pussy."

His freaky sex talk makes me want him even more. My body sails off into the ocean, I am dying … I am exploding.

"Whit," I scream. "Whit…Whit…Whit." Until I can't squeal anymore.

At this same time Whit buckles on top of me. "Ahhhh," he shouts, as his dick convulses, splashing his seed inside the condom. And yet some perverse part of me wishes his gobs of cum were bathing the head of my womb instead.

Chapter 11

Whit

Never in my wildest dream did I ever imagine I could feel this way about a woman.

I have fallen fucking hard for Khloe. The last thing I would have expected.

There is no doubt I am addicted to her, in more ways than one. I laugh at her corny jokes and we tickle each other and play around like children. Me, Whit, behaving like a love-sick puppy? Get the fuck outta here.

She tells me about herself; about growing up with a rich father, her mother having died giving birth to her, and my heart weeps at her misfortune. Her dad became the apple of her eye and he treated her like a princess. When he died, a piece of her heart died with him.

It's been a week since we have been cooped up in the warehouse and I know it's time to move on.

It's never safe to stay in one place for too long.

But it's silly to think that we can run and hide forever. Soon, we will have to face the music. We can't keep doing this for much longer. Someone is bound to spot us.

Khloe finally opens up to me one night after a bout of torrid fucking. "I don't want to keep running," she says, her face drenched with sweat and cum juice coating the inside of her thighs.

"And I don't want to force you to," I reassure her.

Somehow, the longer I have her in my care, the more her innocent warmth melts the ice around my heart and I feel myself changing. The monster is dying and in its stead is a man, hopelessly in love and willing to go to the ends of the earth to shield the woman I adore.

If I die to protect her, then it's the most meaningful death I can ever have.

I know I can't let her die with me, but I'm not sure I can bear to leave her behind when it's time for me to take her somewhere where she'll be safe, knowing that I'll be walking away to a bitter end.

I don't know...I just don't know. And this is the price I knew I would have to pay if ever I broke the Hitman's Code.

So I start exploring ways I can stash her in a safe place; somewhere where she'll be protected. There's an unspoken resolution that I will have to leave her, as I believe that's the only way to truly protect her.

There will always be danger where I'm involved, so I hatch a plan to lead her to safety, while I return to the only life I know; that of kill or be killed.

I can't tell Khloe about these plans, however, because our feelings for each other have grown so strong, that I know, or at least suspect, that she'll refuse, saying she'd rather be in danger than let me continue living the way I used to in the past.

So I begin to love her even more fiercely, intending to live every moment I have with her to its fullest, while I still have the chance.

I put the harsh man I am on the back burner for a while, and begin doting over her, showing my love in many small ways, keeping her happy and contented until the dreaded moment of departure arises.

These idyllic days with Khloe make me feel more alive than all the years I have been roaming this planet, aimlessly. She has given me a new meaning in life. Yes, I am becoming more addicted to her presence.

***

"Let's go out on the town tonight," Khloe moans into my ears, her tongue pressing against my lobes.

I push her away with a start, appalled that she even dares suggest such a notion. "You know it's not safe," I snort, brushing strands of hair from across her face.

It's been two weeks since we disappeared and we have changed safe houses twice, just to throw anyone hunting us off our tracks.

"We've both been cooped up for so long, doing nothing but running and hiding and more running." She makes a face. "There's been no opportunity for either of us to savor the fresh air." She punches my arm playfully. "Let's go out and have some fun, just this once?"

I again shake my head. "It's too dangerous."

"Whit, I know you can handle this. You are accustomed to staying undercover for long periods, but sweetie, it's getting to me... it's driving me crazy," she whines, batting her lashes and peering at me with those puppy-dog eyes.

"Okay, okay." I finally agree, just to shut her up. "I'll take you out tomorrow. Let's go have some fun."

I know she is just not used to this sort of existence and although I have tried my best to make her happy, the lifestyle is starting to bring her spirits down.

I've already arranged to meet an old friend to discuss an arrangement that will bring Khloe to safety, so I decide to take her with me under the cover of simply taking a day off with no strings attached. And why not, I know I will enjoy a date with her too. There is an element of danger involved, but with Khloe developing the symptoms of cabin fever, it's something we have to do.

Besides, the way she looks now, there is almost no chance of anyone recognizing my lover.

Chapter 12

Khloe

Man alive, we are finally out of the safe house and not just driving from one to the other.

Phew.

Whit has kept me pretty much sheltered; alternating between Brooklyn and The Bronx, because he feels it's too great a risk to be caught on the highway trying to get to another state. He knows the highway patrols will be gunning for us, so he plays it safe.

Today, he has taken me to Brooklyn, and we are seated inside a nicely decorated café, where I order a cappuccino and cake. There is no denying my sweet tooth this time around, and my man is keen to indulge me.

"You know Whit, you can be such a sweetheart when you really want to." I gush, looking into his gorgeous eyes.

He looks at me suspiciously. "You don't fucking say," he retorts. "Don't get used to it though." He smiles back at me, melting my heart in the process. "I'm still a tough guy, you know. Don't you dare think I'm getting soft."

I slide my tongue over my lips suggestively. "I know there's no chance of you getting soft, if you know what I mean," I tease.

Whit leans back in his chair, his eyes scan the room, and then roam outside for a minute. Even while enjoying himself, he is making sure the surroundings are safe.

I raise my brow. "Whit...forget our problems for a while, let's just enjoy the day."

"Force of habit," he grunts, rubbing his hand against his now stubbed cheek. "This is how I have managed to stay alive all these years, by taking nothing for granted, no matter how normal they may seem."

Reaching across the table, I take hold of his hands, gently caressing them. "Well, you are doing a superb job with me and that's the reason why I'm crazy about you."

"That's all?" he asks jokingly. "And here I was thinking it was because of my big cock."

My cheeks immediately blush and my eyes flop downwards, afraid to make contact with his. Whit has this raw side to him that I am getting unaccustomed to, but that's what makes him even more exciting and such a turn-on.

"No answer?" He continues, knowing full well the impact his words are having on me.

For a moment I am at a loss for words. "Yes... yes...Whit, I love your huge cock." There, I can't believe I said that.

I have always been shy and reserved. When my girlfriends at college were bragging about their nightly sexcapades, all I did was smile. Guess that's just my DNA.

With Whit, sex is so exciting. He likes to take charge and knows all the right areas to touch and lick. He is a master in bed or any other part of the house in which he chooses to make love to me.

And his dick! Oh my goodness, it's so big...it fills me up every time.

"Daydreaming about me, again?" Whit needles me.

"I was not." I pout, before breaking out into peals of laughter. "Come on, let's take a stroll outside. I need some exercise after all the cake I just ate."

Whit glances around for a few minutes before seizing my hand and leading me outside. I lean my head against his shoulder and all seems right with the world. He caresses my newly shortened hair as we stroll in the shadows, leaning over to look into my eyes.

Every time Whit's eyes move to mine, I fall deeper and deeper in love with him. What a funny thing this feeling called love is, you never know when it will hit you and it does so at the most unexpected moments.

We spend the afternoon having an enchanting time drinking coffee, walking, and talking about things we never knew about each other. "So what are your other passions?" I ask.

He is silent for a moment, deep in thought. "Funny enough, I love to read and I am an avid sports fan, especially the NBA… even though the Knicks aren't winning," he laughs. "I like kids too, but I'm not sure if that will ever happen. I mean, how could I bring a kid into my world?"

Close to the end of the day, Whit sends me off to browse at clothes while he meets with his friend. "There is a colleague I have to meet alone, around the corner," he says, guardedly. "So go do some window shopping. Mark you, don't buy anything, in case anyone asks for identification, ok?"

He draws me close and kisses my lips with

the passion of a man unsure when he will get that chance again. Finally, he lets go and I watch his sexy ass disappear onto the street around the corner.

While Whit's busy meeting with his friend, I have time to indulge in one of my favorite pastimes, window shopping. It sucks that I can't buy anything, but at least I am out of the house and able to browse around stores.

I find myself wondering what it would be like to live a double-life. What if I gave up being who I am and become a different person; Wearing a sleek black bob, bold colored makeup, and a fierce sense of style that makes nobody want to mess with me?

What if I turned into Whit's bad bitch? I mean, kill off the shy little Khloe, and live a high voltage life with him?

Shucks, I know that I'd never be suited to that kind of personality, and Whit's certainly not asking me to change who I am, heaven's forbid. But I can't help but feel that maybe if I could suddenly be tough and hard-nosed I'd stand a better chance at being able to stay with Whit. This is the sort of woman he could really love...someone more like himself.

In my bones, I can feel that there are things he isn't telling me, I guess it has something to do with what he thinks is in my best interest. Darn, I'm worried about *his* best interest. I have to be selfish about the man I love. I don't want him to leave me. I'd rather stay with Whit and accept the risks and the danger that comes with his territory, than leave him behind, forever.

Chapter 13

Whit

Frank is standing in the shadows, just to the left of the store. He looks around nervously before signaling me over. "Long time no see, my friend." I shake his hand vigorously, happy to see a familiar face.

He is an old army buddy who now operates on the outside of the law and can provide anything for a price. However, like everyone else, he does not know that I am a hitman. You're looking good, Whit. Life sure as hell is treating you well." The heavyset black man, dressed in jeans, polo shirt, and a pullover, greets me warmly.

"I'm not doing too badly," I retort. "But man, let's get straight to business."

Frank eyes me curiously, but shrugs, his movement betraying a slight limp, the remnant of a bullet he took in the leg during a firefight in Afghani-stan. "Everything's ready to go," he snorts. "We can pick up the girl and bring her to a sanctuary as early as daybreak, if you are ready."

I smile. The plan is for Frank to have a couple of his goons pick up Khloe and smuggle her out of the country, down to the Caribbean in a small private jet. His guys have everyone on the island in their back pockets, so it's an easy gig. The only difficulty now is to get Khloe to agree. She can be pigheaded and stubborn when she wants to.

"Great. I will let you know when I am ready." I embrace Frank, who quickly disappears into the crowd of pedestrians. The guy is a freaking ghost. That's how we spooks have all managed to survive for so long.

I stroll back toward Khloe with mixed emotions. Watching her gorgeous frame peering through a store window warms my heart and I suddenly feel a sense of remorse. I have gotten so accustomed to having her around. It will be difficult sending her away, but I know it's for the best. It's also tough because I have fallen hopelessly in love with her. Hopelessly addicted to her.

So I sneak up behind her and trap her in a bear hug. "Unfair." Khloe squints her eyes.

"You are looking so darn sexy that I want to fuck you now," I growl.

"Where would you?" she asks incredulously, her eyes brimming with surprise but showing a tinge of lust. "I don't see any hotels around?"

I take her hand and lead her toward the boutique. Her eyes are wild and puzzled. Once inside, I tell the sales agent that we want a private changing room where Khloe can try on some expensive dresses and lingerie. The agent smiles, obviously at the thought of making a good commission, and leads us toward a back room. "She can change in here. Look at anything you are interested in and I will be happy to find your size," she informs us.

Khloe still has a bewildered expression on her face, so I place my fingers on her lips for her to be quiet. I wink, licking my lips. "Just select some sexy lingerie."

She hops around the store, selecting a few pieces, before disappearing into the changing room.

I wait until the sales agent has left to attend to other clients then I open the door to the changing room and step inside, ready to enjoy a bout of naughtiness with Khloe.

What I see inside causes me to gasp, my jaws pop open, pupils enlarge and my mouth goes fucking dry.

Khloe is facing me in a white bustier and skimpy panties. Her magnificent, bountiful curves are almost causing the slinky garments to burst at the seams. The imprint of her camel toe on the crotch of her panties has my cock springing to attention.

I'm fucking horny, to say the least.

"Whit, what are you doing in here?" She tries to cover herself with her hands. "What if someone catches you?"

"I don't give a damn. I want to fuck you right here…right now." I croak, barely able to speak.

I stare at her once again. Khloe has such a luscious body that her curves almost seem unreal. Her breasts are large, ripe, and stiff, popping out of the too-small bustier.

"Whit." She finally looks at me with a hint of mischief in her eyes. They are twinkling with lust and desire at the realization that I have every intention of fucking her raw in the changing room. "Do you like me in this one?"

The sight of her thick body has my cock hard as iron. "Of course… you know I do," I hear myself saying in such a raspy, guttural tone, that I hardly recognize my own voice. I having been wanting to pump my cock into her all day and now that I am about to have her, I am almost ready to nut in my pants.

In a flash, I move closer. Outside, I hear the murmur of voices as customers go about the shopping. Khloe's eyes are burning with lust and in an instant the woman I have become addicted to reaches over, grabs me by the neck, and burns me with a kiss. Her lips part and she adores my mouth with her tongue as we bite, suck and lick each other's lips. This is a new side of the normally reserved woman that I know. "I am hot for you, Whit," she whispers, sticking her tongue into my ears. "The thought of you fucking me in here while people are a few meters away has me horny as fuck."

I am lost in her scent… that of a woman aroused…Her sexual aroma fills up the room, captivating me, and causing my cock to lurch. She resumes our French kissing, her tongue forcing its way into my mouth, seeking mine. I respond. Our tongues twist and turn, battling each other.

Khloe pulls away and stares into my eyes, her breathing rushing out in fiery breaths. "I love fucking in public," I breathe a confession. "And today I need to fuck you raw up in here. Can you handle that?"

My core weeps with the need to possess this woman with the body of a sex bomb, but who is just experiencing her sexual awakening. My pulse is slamming into my eardrum and my already hard cock stiffens even further at an alarming rate. "Yes, I can handle it," Khloe sighs. "So are going to fuck me hard?"

I reach over and grab her by the ass, roughly pulling her toward me. My mouth roams down her neck and my teeth nibble at her jugular, causing her body to convulse. "Fuck, Whit, you are making my pussy clench so hard," she hisses. "Please hurry up and fuck me till I cum."

My hands sink into her big ass cheeks and I clamp down harder on her neck. A stifled moan escapes her pouty, succulent lips, and she bites her bottom lip to keep from crying out. My fingers gently pinch her rock-hard nipples and she shivers in the throes of passion. "Sorry, we don't have time for much foreplay. I have to fuck your sweet pussy right now," I plead, a sense of urgency filling my voice.

Khloe nods and I back her up against the wall, sliding the crotch of her thongs to the side. Raising her hips off the floor, I grab her ass and use my hands underneath the cheeks for support, as I brace her against the wall. I gently nozzle the head of my cock against her clit and feel her stiffen, then continue my motion and feel her wetness splashing against my dick.

Khloe is on fire, gyrating against my dick, trying to force it inside her. But I tease her a bit, continuing to rub against her wetness before gently slipping the head of my dick inside… screwing her… grinding her. She lets out a gasp as if about to cum.

With one sharp thrust, I plunge inside her with all my might. Khloe's eyes roll in the back of her head and she grunts. I place my hand over her mouth and begin pumping her sweet, tight pussy. This time there is no gentleness as she stands on tiptoes and arches her back.

My big, beautiful woman sinks her teeth into my shoulder to keep from screaming, as I pump my dick in and out of her now steaming cunt. Again, I marvel at her tightness. Her insides feel almost silky and her warm juice bathes my cock. I have to fight the urge to flood into her, but I'm not ready for that.

My dick is large and forceful, enjoying the sweetness of her tight box, her warm juices, and the motion of her ass. "Fuck me, Whit… fuck me," Khloe pants in my ears, before again sinking her teeth into my shoulders, this time drawing blood. Her passion spurs me on and I bang her with all my might. She is fucking me back, matching my gyrations and force. Her head is thrown back, and she is grunting so hard I begin to think someone outside must be overhearing us. Not that I give a fuck. Finally, I feel her shudder against me as an orgasm surges through her body... her sex milking me. But I continue my thrusts, wanting to take her over the edge, again... and again.

Khloe climaxes with hurricane-like force and holds onto me for support. I quickly slip out of her, put on my clothes, and beat a hasty retreat before we are interrupted. Minutes later she exits the changing room with a smug smile on her face. I pay the bill and we both leave the store laughing, hand in hand.

"I love you, Whit," Khloe says once we are outside the store, tears welling in her eyes.

"I love you too," I reply honestly.

****

Just when I thought things were looking up, the shit hit the fan.

Someone in Frank's organization has been compromised.

Information that a man was trying to smuggle a woman out of Brooklyn and the country was sure to fetch big bucks at a time when the mob was laying out lots of cash for any information on Khloe's whereabouts.

The streets outside are crawling with cops and assassins, and to make it worse they now have my description.

The bastard Jason Gray is now closing in, so I decide to keep Khloe hidden away in the current safe house and confront the man himself, before he can find us and hurt her.

But when I tell Khloe of my plan, she refuses to let me go. "No way will I allow you to do that, baby," she sobs in my arms. "Because I'm crazy in love with you now and I don't want you to die."

"Nothing's going to happen to me." I try to reassure her. "I'm a big boy and I can take care of punks like your husband."

Khloe looks at me tenderly, her eyes brimming with tears. "Whit, I know you like to think that you're Superman," she scolds. "You are just one man and most likely you won't be able to make it out of this situation alive."

I sweep her off her feet, tall and curvy as she is, and kiss her fears away. If it were any other time but now, I would lay her down on the floor and fuck her, but duty calls.

Eventually, I release her and she looks at me lovingly. "Okay, have it your way," Khloe sighs and retreats toward the bedroom.

'I'm going to lock the door behind me," I shout as she disappears. "There is a sheet of paper on your bedside table with instructions on who to call and when, so you'll be safe, just in case I'm late in returning."

The last thing I hear as I leave the room is the sound of Khloe sobbing in the distance.

Chapter 14

Khloe

I've learned a lot since being on the run with Whit. Not only how to defend myself, but how to be tough and fearless. If Whit thinks I have accepted the fact that he will face my no-good husband alone, he has another thing coming.

He has taught me so much about survival… too much to let a locked room stop me.

I rummage through my purse until I find a paperclip that I use to pick the lock to the bedroom door. Then I recover the gun he gave me for emergencies and rush through the door, ready to save my man from what I'm sure is going to be a bloody and unnecessary demise.

Once outside the safe house, I scan the surrounding environment just as Whit had taught me, to make sure no one suspicious was hanging around.

How can I find him, though? I note the number

written on the piece of paper he left with me and use the burner cell to call. "Yes?" A man's voice answers gruffly on the other end of the line.

"This is your package. I need to find Whit, urgently." My heart is careening in my chest, but I take a deep breath and keep my composure.

"That was not our instructions. We were told you would call us if you needed to be transported somewhere else," the man snarls. "Whit was very specific."

"Listen, Mr. whoever-your-name-is," I snap. "His life is in danger and I need to talk to him now."

I'm about to lay into him when a powerful pair of hands grab me around the neck and another seizes my arms, sending the phone splattering to the ground. One of the men promptly steps on the instrument, squashing it.

I struggle, but they are too strong. A car quickly drives up to the scene and they shove me roughly inside.

Everything is happening so fast around me. All I can see are the faces of men I don't recognize. "Drive," one man orders and the car speeds away.

I should have listened to Whit. I'm not as stealthy, clever, or experienced as he is, and now I have been caught by the very people I meant to confront.

Shoved in the back of the car, I have time to reflect on my life and current situation. The ride seems like an eternity before the car finally slows down and two of the men alight and pull me out. "You prick," I lash out. "Take your filthy hands off me."

The men merely laugh and roughly drag me into what looks like a deserted building. Inside the place is dark at first, but when my eyes finally adjust to the dim light, I make out the inside of a warehouse. There is an eerie feel to the building, with the stench of death hanging in the air.

They toss me ahead of themselves into a large room and I look up to see a slightly beaten up Whit in a corner and Jason, my husband, and another man in front of him holding a large knife. "So look who we have here," Jason snarls. "My lovely wife has decided to join the party."

My eyes dart towards him. If looks could kill, Jason would be dead right now.

I notice Whit's mortified gaze. I know he thought I was safe, but I could not bear the thought of living without him. "You sick son-of-a-bitch," I explode. "How could you do this to me…for what… money?"

"Yes, lots of money." Jason laughs. "And more assets than you can imagine."

As angry as I am, there is still one question I need to be answered. "So did you have my dad killed too?"

Jason's eyes cloak with evil. "Yes, my naïve little wife. We had buildings we wanted to take over to construct a mall, but your dad would not play ball, saying that he didn't want to uproot the poor local people. Can you fucking believe that?"

If I had hated Jason before, I loathe him now.

My eyes turn towards Whit, trying to give him a silent signal. He peers at me, a defiant look on his face.

Jason walks over towards a large table in the corner of the room and retrieves an envelope. "Now, my dear wife," Jason's tone becomes eerily serious. "If you value your life, you will sign these legal documents to turn over all your assets to me."

I am no fool…once I sign those papers, he will kill us both. The situation has now escalated to a point where it seems that escape is impossible, but what my husband and his henchmen don't realize is that I have Whit's gun, hidden away on my body, just in case an emergency like this would arise.

Jason and his cronies are so confident they have us beat that they release me, intending to have me sign the documents. Pretending to resign myself to my fate, I reach inside my bra and pull the gun from its hiding place. "None of you bastards move," I hiss, in a voice so foreign that I myself don't even recognize.

One of the men tries to grab me, but I squeeze off a round into his chest and he sinks to the floor. The other man goes for his gun, but I am too fast for him and drop him too, leaving Jason to cower in a corner.

I rush over to Whit. "Are you okay, darling?" I ask, relief washing over my core.

"Just a few scratches," he replies, taking the gun away from me and advancing toward Jason. "You know what's coming now," he barks at Jason. "The law of the jungle is killed or be killed, and you, Mr. Gray, are now a dead man."

Whit raises the gun and is about to fire, when I jump up, stopping him in his tracks. "Whit, no," I shout. "Don't kill him."

"What do you mean, don't kill him?" Whit looks at me incredulously. "A few minutes ago he was going to kill both of us. I want to make sure he'll never be able to follow us again."

"No, there is another way," I reassure an angry Whit.

Walking over to Jason, I look at the face I once thought handsome. "I should kill you, but I won't become like you. I am different," I scold.

I pull on my finger and remove the ring that I was still wearing and place it in his hand. "Listen very carefully now, Jason," I say in measured tones "I plan on disappearing...the old Khloe is dead, so let her rest in peace."

Whit looks at me and shakes his head. He takes the weapon from my hand and pumps two shots into Jason's head, blood splattering on the wall. "I'm sorry, love, but Jason would never leave us alone. I had to kill him. Plus, he was responsible for your father's death."

As shocked as I am by Whit's action, I know me is right. "So we'll disappear down the islands then, my love." I plant a kiss on his lips. "Because all I really care about anyway is being able to love you. The money is just a bonus and I have lots of it hidden away in Swiss bank accounts."

Whit's eyes narrow and a wry smile forms across his handsome face. "I'm not the silly little girl Jason thought I was, you know. Did he think he would just inherit all I have?"

"Well...I have a few bucks stashed away as well." He pokes me in the ribs. "So let's go somewhere exotic and drink sexy cocktails all day and fuck at nights."

And with all of that behind us, Whit can finally leave the killer inside of him in the dark where he belongs.

Now we can have a different life, somewhere new, with the love that I have found in the most un-likely of places.

Epilogue

Khloe

Four years have passed since Whit and I escaped our past lives to settle in the Caribbean island of the Bahamas.

With Jason gone, we are now safe. No one really knows who Whit is anyway, so we can live our lives in the relative obscurity of the beautiful and exotic island.

Yes, we are now married. I am the proud Mrs. Gavin Morgan, but he will always be Whit to me. Whit, my savior – no other name will do.

We are the proud parents of a beautiful daughter, Sienna, and we could not be happier. Whit and I purchased a small hotel on the island, and it is doing extremely well. Not that we need the money since I am a very wealthy woman and he had a hefty wad of cash stashed away. So we mostly travel the world, as well as play the role of doting parents.

Even today, I find it hard to believe that this caring, loving father was, in another life, a cold-blooded assassin. Yes, Whit is still a tough guy, but around his two girls, he is a teddy bear. He now has the love and support that he never had before and I plan to keep it that way.

Tonight, we are attending a party hosted by some friends of ours on the island. I am having fun sipping on Margaritas and watching the bulky frame of my husband across the room while he chats with a group of men and women. Every now and then he glances in my direction and he breaks out into that sexy smile of his. Even after four years of marriage my heart still thunders in my chest and my pussy clenches when he looks at me.

The party is awesome, but watching Whit's massive thighs in the tight pair of jeans he is wearing has my nipples puckering.

Then, I notice my hunky hubby coming toward me. The man walks with a confident swagger and I go weak in the knees. "I know that look in your eyes." His breaths are coming out in ragged puffs. "I can tell when you are fucking horny."

Listen, when Whit met me I was an innocent virgin. I have since blossomed into a very sexual being, letting my hair down when it comes on to sex with my husband.

His filthy words cause an achy feeling to ride

down my tummy. "You know me only too well," I hiss in his ears. "So what are you going to do about it?"

Whit glances around the room and his mouth curls into a naughty smile. "Come with me," he says gruffly, grabbing me by the hand.

"Whit, where are you taking me?" My pussy is juicing. I know my man. With him, you can never tell his next move. He has a habit of fucking me at the most unexpected time in the most unexpected places. So I allow myself to be led through the large, wooden door.

My husband leads me down a dark street outside the house where he pushes me against a wall. "I am going to fuck you until you scream, woman," he grunts. "I know you want my big cock in your little pussy. You are one naughty girl."

My eyes glaze over and I toss my hair to one side. "You know your wife is obsessed with your cock," I say hoarsely. "From that first time you popped my cherry."

My husband rushes into me cupping both cheeks with his hands, and presses his lips on mine. A lustful feeling steals into my bones and a whimper escapes my lips. My cunt throbs incessantly... yes I am no longer a shy little girl... Seriousness dances in Whit's eyes and I know I am in for a rough ride tonight.

"We don't have a lot of time, people could pass by at any time," he groans into my mouth. Somehow, the thought of discovery has me panting wildly.

My response is to reach for his zipper, pulling it down, and with eager fingers reach inside and grab hold of his erect cock. "Fuck," Whit groans. "I love your soft hands on my cock."

I begin fisting his big, hard dick, feeling it lengthen in my hands and its girth swelling. How I love this enormous cock.

Squatting in front of Whit, I place my tongue on the head of his erection and slowly begin licking. At the same time, I grab onto his balls, causing my husband to let out a roar. "You are going to make me nut in your mouth." He gently eases his dick against my mouth, desperate to get inside. So I oblige by pursing my lips and sucking him into my mouth.

Wrapping his hands in my hair, Whit pumps my mouth. I am choking, but I open my mouth as deep as possible until I can feel the head of his cock in the back of my throat. "Of sweet Lord, I need my cock in your pussy now." However, Whit pushes me away, grabs me, and pushes my head against the wall. Lust swells in my tummy and my legs begin to shake as my hubby pulls up my short skirt until his hands are grasping my ass cheeks. "You have the sweetest ass," he grunts. "And it's all mine."

There are no words to describe how this erotic, public display of sexuality is causing electric shocks to rattle my poor body. He pushes his cock against the crack of my ass, rubbing it against my panties. "Stop playing and fuck me, Whit," I say, annoyed by his playfulness. Then the air is knocked out of my lungs as he pulls my thong to one side and slips the massive head into my now soaking pussy. "Holy fuck," I whimper. "Mr. Hitman, are you going to kill me with that prick tonight?"

Whit responds with a grunt and pumps his cock deeper into me as his finger flicks my clit and all hell breaks loose in my body. I can't help myself so I scream, my voice carrying far in the night air. Whit slaps me on the ass with one hand while he uses the other to grasp my neck. My husband is fucking and choking the shit out of me and I am loving it.

My passion swells and I moan his name over and over. The pleasure draws tight like a rope, taut, aching, as I grind against my sweet cock. "Yes, keep hitting that spot," I cry. "Keep hitting that spot in your pussy and I am going to cum for you." Whit spears into me, riding me high and then low, and a fire sear through my loins, ripping me apart. He pulls his cock all the way out and then pumps deep. "Fuck I am cuming...don't stop, Whit. Fuck me raw."

I am lost in the clouds, luxuriating in the sweet sensation of a toe-curling orgasm. My senses are shattered as I cum over and over, and just when

I think it's all over, I feel a damp finger sliding into my asshole and I die. My legs buck and Whit has to hold on to me to keep me from falling to the ground. Then I feel my cunt clenching on his throbbing cock. "Khloe…Khloe," I hear Whit wailing as he blasts gobs of cum inside my pussy which I accept gleefully.

Finally, he ceases his pumping and hisses against my neck. "I will never, ever let you go," he says sharply. "I am addicted to you."

"You would not get rid of me husband, I would have to kill you first."

We both laugh, pull ourselves together and head back to the party wrapped in each other's arms.

My man keeps telling me he is addicted to me and I plan to keep it that way.

Who says life doesn't have a happy ending?

Epilogue - Addicted

Whit

They say people can change, and I am a testament to that fact.

I never thought I had it in me to settle down, but I have. I have found the woman of my dreams. A woman who I am addicted to and all of a sudden everything is right with the world.

I am addicted to her smile. The way her eyes light up when she is happy and how they droop when she is sad.

I am addicted to the way she walks, swinging her sweet ass from side to side; a sensuous glide that wrecks me every time.

But most of all, I am addicted to the woman she is – a gentle soul; and although she is loving and kind, she has warped into a tough businesswoman and a tigress sexually.

The other half of my beloved family, my

daughter, is the apple of my eye and I can't wait to get home in the evenings to spend time with her.

Khloe...Yes, I am addicted to you and I will protect you for as long as I live.

THE END

A MESSAGE FROM KYLIE HUDSON

Thank you so much for reading WHIT and KHLOE'S book. I hope you enjoyed your journey into the life of this bad boy alpha male and his woman. If you enjoyed this book, please consider leaving a review. **Reviews help authors like me stay visible and help bring others to my book.**

Books By This Author

Billionaire's Dark Passion

He is accustomed to getting what he wants.
And now he wants her.

CAIDEN TALON is a cold, heartless bastard.
He simply loves the ladies and then leaves them after a few hours of passion.
That's why they call him "Mr. One Night Stand".
Redwood Tree tall, chiseled body, bulging biceps, and a massive chest that seems to reach all the way to his neck.
Caiden's a dominant, cocky bad boy with a canon between his legs.
He's the ultimate Alpha Male.
An untimely incident forces him to give up his life of racing fast cars and chasing fast women.
Now he is the billionaire head of a Fortune 500 company with a point to prove.
But he has a deep, dark, sexual secret that threatens to destroy his perfect world.

They say opposites attract.

Enter shy and reserved young writer Emmanuella Porter, but with a thick curvy body and the face of an angel that drive all the men wild with lust.

For her scoring an interview with the macho billionaire is a chance of a lifetime. Her ticket to the top.

But she finds Caiden a cocky, macho prick. And so full of himself.

So why does her heart beat faster and heat rises between her legs every time he is near?

Will she fall for this modern-day Alpha or will Caiden's deep, dark secret be too much for her to handle?

Billionaire's Dark Passion is a steamy standalone, BWWM BBW Alpha Male Romance with a HEA ending.

Caiden Talon is the bad boy alpha you have been waiting for, while Emmanuella's coming of age proves the perfect foil.

Absolutely no cliffhangers.

If you enjoy this Interracial and Multicultural Romance please leave a review because it will help other potential readers.

His Sweet Temptation

After the tragic death of his fiancée 'The Giant' Parker Brady has promised to never love again.

Skyscraper tall with rippling muscles and chiseled features that make women swoon, he will romance them as long as there are no romantic entanglements.

He has no time for commitments.

But Parker is a Dominant Alpha Male and accustomed to getting what he wants – by any means necessary.

And when he sets eyes on a feisty, ravishing dark and beautiful college student, bedding her is all that's on his mind.

This thick, curvy, goddess-like siren makes his heart race and the blood run hot in his veins.

A chance date leaves his wanting more, much more Brainy college student LONDON SPENCER is sweet and voluptuous. But all that's on her mind is acing her exams and getting a good job and take her struggling mother and sister out of poverty.

She doesn't have time for boys, or romance for that matter.

But after meeting the hunky, hulking Parker why does she feel all swoony and there is that clenching between her thighs whenever he is near?

But there are dark forces at work that threaten Parker's empire and any chance of finding true love again.

London has never met a man like the Dominant billionaire financier. Will destiny bring two such different individuals together?

His Prize Sweet Temptation is a standalone, Billionaire BWWM Alpha Male BBW Romance Book, filled with steamy and sexy scenes, but with a HEA end-

ing.
Absolutely no cliffhangers

Billionaire's Fake 90 Day Fiancee

Billionaire RYKER DEAN is the ultimate Alpha Male. Skyscraper tall, and with a body wrapped with corded muscles.
But when it comes to women he is ice-cold, and never sticks around for any length of time.
A Dominant, he doesn't play by the book, but uses any means necessary to get what he wants.
But when a long-time friend, a man who saved his life, calls in a favor, he simply can't refuse.
Now he faces the ultimate test – playing the role of a fake fiancée.
But when he meets his fake wife-to-be, all bets are off and the playbook goes out the window.
A woman that makes his heart race and the blood run hot in his veins.

SIENA is thick and curvy.
A big, beautiful black woman, with a penchant for turning heads wherever she goes.
Now her stepdad has placed her in a rather compromising position; a fake engagement to a man she finds cocky and totally full of himself.
Yet why does acrobats does somersaults in her tummy and that tingle starts between her thighs whenever he is near?

How will this fake romance play out?
Billionaire's Fake 90 Day Fiancée is a standalone, BWWM Alpha Male BBW Romance Book, filled with steamy and sexy scenes, but with a HEA ending. Absolutely no cliffhangers.

Billionaire's Dark Romance

A standalone, steamy, Alpha Male romance.

Introducing a new type of Alpha male
From the outside, it would appear Lucas Steele has it all.

He commands a billion dollar empire, drives million dollar sports cars and dresses the part. Add his sculpted physique, chiseled jaw and piercing eyes and he is the envy of the Hollywood Hills Jet Set.

But he has never known the love of a woman and that's the one risk he dares not take.

Kenya Masters is a super smart, gorgeous, voluptuous, thick and sexy NYU College Junior, who has men falling over themselves to sample her bountiful treasures...and the only woman who dares to resist Lucas.

But Kenya has her own dark sexual secret.... a smoldering, desire that she is waiting on the right man to explore.

Billionaire's Dark Romance is the second in the Hunks of Hollywood series. It's a Billionaire BWWM, Alpha Male, Bad Boy BBW Romance with no cheating and a HEA. It however, contains steamy, sexy scenes.
Read this complete full-length standalone romance from start to finish right now by scrolling back and clicking "BUY NOW".